THE GIRL WHO LEAPT
THROUGH TIME

THE GIRL WHO LEAPT THROUGH TIME

YASUTAKA TSUTSUI

Translated by David Karashima

ALMA BOOKS

ALMA BOOKS LTD
3 Castle Yard
Richmond
Surrey TW10 6TF
United Kingdom
www.almabooks.com

The Girl Who Leapt through Time and *The Stuff that Nightmares Are Made of*
first published by Alma Books Ltd in 2011
Reprinted 2017
Original titles: 'Toki o Kakeru Shōjo' and 'Akumu no Shinso' from
Toki o Kakeru Shōjo
Copyright © Yasutaka Tsutsui, 1967
Toki o Kakeru Shōjo originally published in Japan in 1967 by Seikosha and
republished in 2009 by Kadokawa Shoten Co. Ltd., Tokyo
English translation © David Karashima, 2011
All rights reserved.

Front-cover design: Jem Butcher
Cover image: Getty Images

Printed in Great Britain by CPI Group (UK) Ltd, Croydon CR0 4YY

ISBN: 978-1-84688-134-3

Contents

THE GIRL WHO LEAPT THROUGH TIME   7

THE STUFF THAT NIGHTMARES ARE MADE OF   107

THE GIRL WHO LEAPT THROUGH TIME

THE DARK SHADOW IN THE SCIENCE LAB

It had been hours since most of the students had left the school building. Its halls and classrooms were now cold, and everywhere was quiet, except for the distant sound of someone playing Chopin's 'Polonaise' on the piano in the auditorium.

Kazuko Yoshiyama was in her last year of junior high school, and she'd just about finished cleaning up the science lab with her classmates, Kazuo Fukamachi and Goro Asakura.

"That's good enough. I'll take out the trash," she said. "You boys can go wash your hands."

As the tall and lanky Kazuo left the room with the short and stocky Goro, Kazuko had to stop herself from letting out a chuckle at the contrast between her two friends. They were very different in other ways too. Both of them were very clever, that was for sure. But while Goro worked hard and could be very impulsive, Kazuo was a bit of a dreamer. In fact, he often seemed to be in a world of his own, and Kazuko could never be sure of what he was thinking.

While washing their hands in the bathroom sink, Goro looked over at Kazuo.

"Kazuko's cute, and she's nice, too. But she can be a little overbearing at times, can't she?"

Goro liked to pepper his sentences with big words from time to time.

"Oh yeah?" said Kazuo, who had been miles away again. "What makes you say that?"

"Don't you think she can be overbearing?" said Goro, puffing up his chest to match his face, which was always rather red and puffy. "She treats us like we're kids. Come on. *You boys can go and wash your hands,* she says."

"I hadn't really thought about it," replied Kazuo, who already appeared to be setting off on another excursion in his mind.

Kazuko took the trash out to the back of the building and came back to the small science lab to put away some brooms they'd been using. But as she placed her hand on the doorknob, she thought she heard a sound coming from inside.

"That's odd," thought Kazuko.

Although it was called the small science lab, the room was generally used as a storage space and was filled with lots of interesting things like jars of biological samples, skeletons, stuffed animals and all kinds of chemicals. For most of the girls in the school, the room was a creepy place best avoided. But Kazuko wasn't the sort of person to mind.

"Nobody should be in here," said Kazuko to herself. "I wonder if it could be Mr Fukushima?"

But then, she'd seen her teacher leave earlier through another door, so it surely couldn't be him making the noise. So who could it be? Kazuko started to feel a little scared. But nevertheless, she managed to summon up the courage to open the door. But as soon as she did, there was a great smash, and the sound of breaking glass echoed around the walls of the room.

"Who's there?" said Kazuko, her voice wavering as she struggled to see in the dark.

She could just about see that there were some test tubes lined up along a desk in the middle of the room, and it seemed that one of those had simply rolled off onto the floor, leaving a pool of liquid to spread across the tiles. Someone must have been doing an experiment in here, she thought. But who? And where on earth did they go?

Kazuko walked over to the desk to read the labels on the bottles of chemicals lined up next to the test tubes. But before she could, a dark shadow jumped out from behind the chemicals cabinet and scuttled behind a partition next to the door. Kazuko froze. Could it be a burglar?

"Who's there?" she called out. "Stop scaring me like that, and show yourself!"

The door leading to the hallway rattled.

"It's no use trying to escape to the hall!" yelled Kazuko, trying hard to stop her fear from overwhelming her. "That door is locked!"

When Kazuko's voice had echoed away, the room fell back into silence. With no more rattling of the door and not a sound from behind the partition.

"I know who you are!" said Kazuko, feeling a little more brave. "Come out Kazuo! Or Goro! I know it's one of you two trying to scare me!"

Kazuko waited for a response, but none came. So instead, she gulped down her fear and tiptoed over to the partition. Then she stopped, took a quiet breath, and slowly peered around the edge. But incredibly, there was nobody there.

THE SCENT OF LAVENDER

"What just happened?" gasped Kazuko, incredulously.

Was that someone's shadow she'd seen? She was sure of it. There was no way it could have been an illusion. No, she was sure she'd seen somebody move behind the partition.

Kazuko reached for the door that led to the hallway and tried pulling it. But, just as she thought, it was locked. So whoever had been here clearly hadn't left through there. So where had they gone? They couldn't have just vanished. That would be ridiculous. But what other explanation was there?

Completely confused, Kazuko slowly returned to the desk where the test tubes were lined up. There was a slight hint of a sweet scent in the air, and Kazuko assumed it must be coming from the contents of the broken test tube. And though she wasn't quite sure what the scent was, she did notice that it was quite pleasant. In fact she could remember smelling this before somewhere. It was something sweet and nostalgic. But what was it?

She reached for one of the bottles of chemicals on the desk and tried to read the label. But it was too dark for her to see properly. She tried squinting to see if that helped, but as she did, she started to feel light-headed. That sweet smell was growing stronger by the second until – all of a sudden – it overpowered her, sending her crumbling to the floor and into unconsciousness.

A few minutes later, Kazuo and Goro returned to the science lab.

"Come on, Kazuko. Let's go!" called out Kazuo.

"We've got your bag here!" Goro added in a loud voice as he pushed open the door to the main lab. But the lab was empty.

"I guess she hasn't got back from taking out the trash yet. Probably ran into someone and is still out there chatting away. Girls just love to talk!"

"I doubt it," said Kazuo, in his usual relaxed way, as he pointed to the door of the smaller lab. "She's probably in there putting away the brooms."

Goro walked off towards the small science lab, swinging his bag and Kazuko's as he went.

"Nope. She's not here." He called out, before suddenly letting out a high-pitched scream.

"What's up?" called Kazuo, running in after to find Goro standing by the side of Kazuko, who was lying still on the floor.

"What's happened?" asked Goro, trembling. "She's not… dead… is she?"

"Don't be ridiculous!" said Kazuo, taking her wrist in his hand and checking her pulse. "She seems fine. Can you grab her legs?"

"What for?"

"So we can carry her to see the nurse, of course! I think she's fainted."

When the three of them reached the nurse's room, there was no one there. So Kazuo and Goro lay Kazuko down on the bed.

"I'll go look for a teacher," said Kazuo. "You open that window and find a way to cool her forehead."

Goro was clearly frightened, and he nodded without a word. Then, after Kazuo had left, he composed himself for a moment, opened the window and dabbed his handkerchief in water before placing it on Kazuko's head.

"It's probably exhaustion," Goro mumbled to himself

sheepishly. "It's ridiculous for them to ask the three of us to clean a room that big!"

"Come on Kazuko! Wake up!" said Goro with tearful eyes as he dabbed the handkerchief in water again and placed it back on her forehead.

Finally, after what seemed like an eternity, Kazuo returned with Mr Fukushima, who'd been the last person left in the staff room.

"Yes, I think she's just fainted," he said after giving her a quick examination.

Together, they waited in silence for several minutes. Then finally it looked as if Kazuko was starting to wake up.

"Oh my. What happened?" she said.

"You fainted in the laboratory," replied Kazuo.

Immediately Kazuko's memory came flooding back, and after taking just a moment to regain her composure, she began to tell the others all about her encounter with the shadowy figure.

"Wow, that's really something," said Kazuo. "But when we found you on the floor, there weren't any test tubes or bottles of chemicals around. And there wasn't anything on the floor either."

"And we didn't smell anything," added Goro.

"Really?" said Kazuko sitting up on the bed, clearly surprised. "That's so strange. I'm sure I… I want to check the room again. Come with me."

Mr Fukushima raised his hand.

"Hey now, not so fast. You should take it easy after fainting like that. Are you sure you're okay?"

"Yes, I'm sure."

"Well, if you're sure, then I will come with you."

Together, they returned to the science lab. But when they got there, sure enough, there was nothing to be seen. Nothing on the table. And not even a shard of glass where the broken test tube had been earlier.

"But that's so odd," said Kazuko in bewilderment.

"That smell you mentioned," asked Mr Fukushima, "could you tell what it was?"

"Well, it was a sweet smell. But how can I describe it…"

Then the answer suddenly dawned on her. "That's it! It was lavender!"

"Lavender?"

"Yes! I remember when I was in elementary school, and my mother used to let me smell her lavender perfume. It was the same smell!"

But Kazuko knew there was something else about the smell. Something she couldn't quite remember. But something that was somehow very important.

RUMBLING AND SHAKING

Kazuko didn't feel her normal self for several days after the incident in the science lab. She wouldn't go so far as to say that she was feeling ill or anything. It was just that her body seemed to have an odd lightness to it, like a sort of floating sensation that left her feeling ungrounded. Like she might suddenly do something crazy. But this strange feeling was more mental than physical, and Kazuko couldn't help but wonder if it might have been caused by the lavender-scented chemical in the laboratory. In fact, she was almost sure of it.

On the third night after the incident, Kazuko finished her homework and climbed into bed at eleven. She'd been playing basketball in the afternoon, and her body was exhausted, but her mind was still sharp and wide awake, so she was having trouble getting to sleep. And as she lay there in bed, staring at the ceiling and thinking of the incident in the lab, there came a great rumbling noise, and Kazuko's bed began jolting up and down.

"Earthquake!" said Kazuko to herself. Within moments the room began shaking sideways and letting out disturbing creaking sounds. This was no minor tremor. This was a big one.

Kazuko had always hated earthquakes. So she jumped out of bed, ran out of her room without changing out of her nightgown and scurried along the hallway, with its windows that were now creaking, too. But the very moment when she opened the front door, the creaking and rumbling came to an abrupt end. Hearing steps behind her, she turned around to see her mother and younger sisters standing in the doorways of their rooms, looking pale and surprised.

"We'd better go in the garden," said Kazuko, "in case there's an aftershock."

And within moments they were all standing shivering in the breeze in the garden. Sure enough, several aftershocks came along within minutes, but they weren't too big. So once they'd decided it was safe again, they all returned to the house and went back to bed. But again, Kazuko found it difficult to sleep. After all, her heart was now racing from all that drama. But after lying there for several minutes more, she felt her eyelids starting to become heavy.

Suddenly, just as she was finally drifting off, there came a loud and piercing scream from the road in front of their house.

"Fire!" came a single voice. Then came the voices of many: "Fire! Fire!"

What were the chances of so many incidents in one night! Kazuko was getting sick of it by now, and felt like crying in frustration. She jumped out of bed again and went over to the window, pushing open the lace curtains that hung there.

Outside, about two blocks away, she could see the chimney of a bathhouse enveloped in smoke. *Oh my goodness!* she thought to herself. *Goro's family store is right next to that bathhouse!*

As two fire engines passed Kazuko's house, their sirens blaring through the night, she hastily pulled a light overcoat on over her nightgown and left her room to investigate.

"Where do you think you're going?" asked her mother from behind the door to her room.

"There's a fire near Goro's house!" she replied. "I'm going to see what's going on."

"Don't be daft! It's too dangerous!"

But Kazuko pretended not to hear her mother's warning. Instead she quickly pulled on her wooden sandals and ran out into the night to where a bunch of onlookers had already gathered. It seemed as if the fire had started near the back door of the bathhouse, so it hadn't spread to the Asakura General Store yet.

"Please, everyone, stay back!" shouted the police at the growing mass of sleepy spectators. "You're getting in the way of the firefighters!"

"I felt an earthquake earlier," said a man standing next to Kazuko to one of his friends. "It must have toppled the gas burner over and started the fire."

"Hey you!" said someone, tapping Kazuko on the shoulder from behind. Kazuko turned to see Kazuo standing there in his pyjamas.

"Oh, Kazuo! I was worried about Goro's shop."

"Me too. But I think everything is fine. I hear it's just a small fire. They said it'll be extinguished in no time," said Kazuo in his characteristically laid-back fashion.

Not too long after, when the last of the flames had been snuffed out by the firefighters, Kazuko and Kazuo walked over to Goro's house. Together they jumped for joy at Goro's lucky escape from the oncoming fire. Then they all went back to their homes.

Kazuko glanced at her clock as she got back into bed yet again. It was already three in the morning. She was absolutely exhausted, and fell asleep within minutes, but she kept having strange dreams all through the night. At first she saw a shadowy figure that jumped out from behind the fire and then flew away. Then she found herself in the lab again, which also started to rumble and shake violently. When she finally woke up, she found herself covered in sweat. But at least it was morning.

She looked over to where the sun's rays were coming in through the window, casting lacy shadows on the floor. *What time is it?* she thought to herself, turning to glance at the clock. *Oh my goodness! I'm late!*

Skipping breakfast, she ran out of the house, with a sleepy, aching head and tired, unsteady legs. Fortunately, she caught sight of Goro waiting at the traffic light.

"Hey Goro!" she called out. "Are you running late, too?"

Goro turned around and smiled, happy that he wasn't the only one running behind today.

"Yeah," said Goro. "It took me so long to fall back to sleep after the fire that I ended up sleeping through my alarm."

When the light turned green, they both dashed across the zebra crossing, but as they reached the middle, an unfamiliar voice startled them.

"Watch out!"

Then came a deafening horn.

Kazuko and Goro turned to see a large truck coming straight towards them. It looked as if it had just run a red light, and now it was heading directly for the intersection where they stood.

Kazuko whipped around and ran straight into Goro, who was standing right behind her – and they both tumbled to the ground. She looked up, and the truck was closer. Then closer still. Until its massive tyres were just meters from her face and Kazuko could do nothing but close her eyes.

BETWEEN DREAM AND REALITY

Kazuko's mind was racing with different scenes and different thoughts. Too many for her to deal with.

I'm going to die! she thought to herself. *Run over by a huge, heavy truck! If only I'd stayed in bed a bit longer. Then I wouldn't be so tired and slow!*

Everything seemed to be moving in slow motion, and she prayed for the safety of her warm and cosy bed back home. But she knew there was nothing she could do. Nothing except keeping her eyes closed as tightly as she could. And so she did. About a second passed. But nothing happened. Then another. But still nothing happened. Kazuko began to wonder what on earth was going on. But right at that moment, she felt herself slipping into unconsciousness. She felt a sense of warmth begin to engulf her. Like the warmth and cosiness of her bed that she'd been praying for.

When Kazuko opened her eyes, she found herself back in her room. She was wearing her nightgown and the sun was streaming in to paint lacy patterns on the floor. Had it all been just a dream? But it felt so real. And she remembered it all so clearly – the car horn, Goro's screams, the shrieks of nearby pedestrians. Too clearly for it to be a dream.

Kazuko was struck by a sudden headache. She looked over at the clock and saw that it was now 7:30. So she had plenty of time for a nice, leisurely breakfast before strolling off to school. That meant she wouldn't be running late and she wouldn't be tired and sleepy – which caused her to be hit by the truck in her dream. And it was a dream, wasn't it? If it wasn't, then time must have turned back, and surely that could never happen.

Kazuko slowly got out of bed. Nothing in the house had changed, and her mother and sisters were all enjoying breakfast together as usual. But despite having plenty of time to eat, Kazuko didn't have much of an appetite. So instead she got ready and left the house right away.

What if this really was the second time for me to leave the house today? she thought to herself. *If just one more strange thing happens today, then surely I'll go mad!* As she reached the crossroads, possibly for the second time, she looked for Goro but couldn't see him. And there was no out-of-control truck either. So she just carried on and made her way to school safely.

She sat down at her desk as she always did and briefly surveyed the classroom. Again, Goro was nowhere to be seen. If only he'd arrive soon, then she could talk to him and find out if the incident with the truck was just a dream or whether there was a chance it might really have happened.

"Morning!" called Kazuo from behind her.

"Oh, morning!" replied Kazuko, considering whether she should tell him all about the incident. Kazuo was a bright individual after all, and might be able to provide some sort of insight. But she quickly decided that it might be better to wait for Goro to arrive so they could all talk about it together.

"Is everything okay?" said Kazuo. "You look a little pale."

Kazuo was always rather attentive, so he often noticed little things like that.

"Oh it's nothing," said Kazuko, shaking her head. "I couldn't sleep much. First because of the earthquake. Then because of the fire! So I'm feeling pretty sleepy today."

"A fire?" said Kazuo. "And an earthquake? I didn't know anything about either of those."

"Are you kidding? There was a big earthquake, and Goro's house nearly caught fire. Don't you remember? We were all in our pyjamas, and we met up in front of Goro's house!"

"We met up? And I was there? Are you sure you weren't dreaming?"

"Dreaming!" retorted Kazuko. "I wasn't dreaming!"

YESTERDAY'S QUESTIONS

Could it really have been nothing more than a dream – the earthquake and the fire in the bathhouse right behind Goro's house? But then, how come Kazuko could remember it all in such sharp detail – the different colours of the flames that leapt up against the night sky, and the exact words of her conversation with Kazuo?

"What's happening to me?" Kazuko said to herself. "My memory is going to pieces!"

"What's that?" said Kazuo.

"It's just I'm sure I ran into you last night."

"No. I'm sure it was a dream," said Kazuo, standing up. "For a moment I wondered if it might be possible that I was sleepwalking – then you could have met me and chatted to me and I wouldn't remember. That would have been weird. But it would have been possible. But then you said I was wearing pyjamas, and I don't actually own any pyjamas."

"Oh," said Kazuko, nodding weakly. "Then I guess it really was just a dream."

But deep down inside, Kazuko couldn't quite believe that was true.

"Morning!" said Goro, putting his bag down beside them.

"Goro," said Kazuo. "Is it true that your house nearly caught fire last night?"

"What?" replied Goro, his back arching and his face turning its characteristic shade of red. "That's not funny. Who would say such a thing?"

"Oh, nobody," said Kazuo. "I thought I heard something like that, that's all."

Kazuko was grateful to Kazuo for saving her from embarrassment. But still her mind was teeming with unanswered questions.

As the first period of math class began, Mr Komatsu – the fat math teacher – wrote down an equation on the board, and Kazuko began to frown. It was the very same problem they'd solved just the day before. But more than that, Mr Komatsu had written the problem on the board at exactly the same time before, and Kazuko had been called to the front of the class, where she'd struggled for some time over the solution.

"It's the same problem as yesterday," mumbled Kazuko to herself, to the surprise of Mariko Koyama, who was sitting next to her.

"What do you mean?" asked Mariko. "Did you know this was going to be today's problem?"

"No, I mean we did this problem yesterday in class. Don't you remember?"

"I don't think so. We didn't do a question like this yesterday. I'm seeing it for the first time."

"No, I have it here in yesterday's notes," added Kazuko, feeling a rush of nervousness as she began to flip through the pages of her notebook. But when she got to yesterday's page, the math problem wasn't written on it. In fact, it was completely blank! Kazuko nearly yelped in surprise. Where was the problem she so clearly remembered writing yesterday? And where was the answer she'd worked so hard to arrive at? It was all so confusing. It was also worrying for Mariko, who sat there in silence as she saw the colour drain from Kazuko's face.

"Okay. Let's see who knows the answer to this one," said Mr Komatsu, his eyes scanning the classroom just as they had the day before. Kazuko couldn't believe her ears, and she felt like the world was spinning around her – Mariko staring at her from the side, Mr Komatsu scanning the class with his shiny glasses, the problem on the blackboard. It was all just too much, so Kazuko closed her eyes.

It's just like yesterday all over again! she thought to herself. *Could it be possible that the teacher would call on her again too?*

"Kazuko. Can you come up and solve this problem?"

"Ye-yes," stammered Kazuko as she stumbled to her feet.

Taking a piece of chalk from Mr Komatsu's outstretched hand, she desperately wrote out the answer she remembered from the day before for all to see. *Maybe this is the dream! She thought. Maybe everything else was real – the earthquake, the fire and the truck. Maybe it was just this part now that was the nightmare!*

"Impressive," said Mr Komatsu, blinking in surprise. "You seemed to breeze through that one."

Kazuko bowed to Mr Komatsu, returned to her seat and leant in close to Mariko.

"Mariko."

"Yes?"

"Today is Wednesday the nineteenth, right?"

"Let me see." Mariko thought about it for a moment before shaking her head. "No, it's Tuesday the eighteenth."

A CRAZY TUESDAY

Kazuko couldn't concentrate on anything for the rest of the day, and the more she tried to understand what was going on, the more confused she became. Had time just slipped back by one day? No, surely that couldn't be! After all, nobody else seemed to have noticed. So did that mean that only Kazuko had gone back one day in time? It would explain a lot of things. But how and why on earth would such a thing happen? Then suddenly, her mind became clear.

Oh no! she thought to herself. *If today really is yesterday, the eighteenth, then doesn't that mean that the earthquake is going to strike tonight? As well as the fire that threatened to destroy Goro's house!* Kazuko's mind was racing, and she pushed away her homework half-done. Then again, she'd already done that homework once, hadn't she? And what did it matter anyway? Surely homework was the least of her problems right now!

Kazuko left the house with no destination in mind, but she was dying to tell someone. At first, she thought about visiting Goro. But then, Goro could be easily scared and was sometimes rash in his behaviour. Perhaps it would be better to visit Kazuo instead? Sure, he came across at times as being a bit spaced out. But underneath it all, Kazuo was really rather smart. So off she went.

It didn't take long for Kazuko to get to Kazuo's fashionable western-style house, with its garden on the right-hand side of the door and its greenhouse full of unusual flowers that always seemed to be in bloom. She took a breath and smelled something sweet. It was the unmistakable scent of lavender!

"That's the scent," said Kazuko to herself as she filled her lungs with air. The flowers all belonged to Kazuo's father, and Kazuko remembered how he'd once shown her all the different kinds he was growing. She remembered he'd told her that lavenders belong to the *Lamiaceae* family, and that they are green all year round. She also remembered that the plant was originally from southern Europe, where its unique scent had made it popular as an ingredient in perfume.

As she stood on the doorstep waiting for someone to

answer the door, Kazuo's window opened, and both Kazuo and Goro poked their heads out.

"Look, it's Kazuko!" said Goro.

"Hey Kazuko!" said Kazuo, "come on up, there's nobody home!"

Kazuko nodded, stepped inside and made her way over to Kazuo's room.

"Is everything alright?" asked Kazuo.

"If there's something bothering you, I'll be willing to help!" added Goro, doing his best to affect a masculine nod.

"Well, yes there is something I'd like to tell you," said Kazuko, taking a seat in front of them.

"Whatever it is, it seems very formal!" said Goro, his back straightening in anticipation.

Kazuko was still not entirely sure she was ready to talk about what was happening. Would they believe her if she did? Probably not. But then, she was getting nowhere trying to think about it all by herself. So she decided to tell them anyway.

"Okay, now, I have something to tell you that is very difficult to believe. So it's hard for me to tell you. But please try to listen to me until the end of my story. And please try not to laugh!"

Kazuko started with the earthquake the night before and ended with what happened in the classroom earlier on. And although she'd expected her friends to giggle all the way through, they sat there listening attentively with bated breath until the very end.

"There," said Kazuko. "That's what I wanted to tell you. I don't care if you believe me or not. I probably wouldn't, if someone else was telling me. But I really did experience everything I just told you. It wasn't a dream. I'm sure of it!"

Kazuo and Goro appeared to be lost in their own thoughts, and Kazuo in particular seemed to be taking this far too seriously to just brush it off as nonsense.

"I really want to believe it," said Goro, breaking the silence. "I want to believe it because it's coming from you, Kazuko. But I can't help but feel there must be some sort of misunderstanding."

"I expected as much," said Kazuko to herself.

"Kazuko!" pleaded Goro, his face turning redder by the minute. "You know what I mean, don't you? I mean, for a whole day to just rewind on itself…"

"Wait a second, Goro," interrupted Kazuo. "Maybe you have some sort of special power!"

"What do you mean, special power?"

"Well, I don't know much about it, but I remember reading somewhere that there are some special people who have the power to transport themselves to other places in the world, just by thinking about it. It's called teleportation. So when the truck was about to hit you, you might have used some power like that to move through time and space – even without knowing it!"

"What? No way! That's ridiculous!" Goro shook his head violently. "That's impossible! So unscientific! It goes against all common sense!"

"But things happen all the time that can't be explained by common sense."

"But there's no evidence, Kazuo!" shouted Goro, annoyed. "Can you prove any of it?"

"I can!" shouted Kazuko in response. "We'll just wait and see if there's an earthquake tonight, and if your house ends up being threatened by fire."

"How can you say such a thing!" shouted Goro, now scarlet with anger.

"I don't mean to be rude," said Kazuko. "But this is the only way to find out if there's any truth to this."

"Of course it isn't true!" said Goro, storming out of the room.

"Now I've made him angry," said Kazuko to Kazuo. "What should I do?"

"I wouldn't worry about it too much," said Kazuo, frowning. "He's not a bad guy, but he needs to learn to control his temper. Besides, you're right. It's the only chance we have for finding out what's happening."

After several minutes had passed, Goro still hadn't returned. So Kazuo stepped out of the room, only to find him leafing through the phone book in the hallway.

"What are you doing?" Kazuo asked.

"Looking for a mental hospital," Goro replied.

"Don't be so nasty to Kazuko!" shouted Kazuo. "Would you really consider having one of your best friends locked up in a lunatic asylum?"

"But…" said Goro angrily, "she's already starting to go mad. If we don't get her to a doctor soon, she might go *completely* nuts!"

"And you can prove that she's mentally sick, can you?"

"I don't have to. Her absurd story is proof enough!"

"But what if it is true? If there really is an earthquake and a fire tonight?"

"No way!"

"It's easy to say that. But we won't know for sure until tonight. So why don't we just wait until tonight and see what happens? If nothing happens, then you can do as you wish. You can call the mental institution first thing in the morning if you like."

"I guess…" agreed Goro, reluctantly.

When she got home from Kazuo's place, Kazuko couldn't think of anything else, and she certainly had no appetite for dinner. After all, the food was exactly the same as the night before, as was the conversation between her mother and younger sisters.

It's just like we're all acting in a play! she thought to herself.

Kazuko couldn't bring herself to do her homework either. She'd already done it the night before, but once again those pages of her notebook were blank. If she really tried, she was sure she could remember her work and write it out again. But she just couldn't bring herself to do that. Instead she decided to get into bed and get some much-needed sleep. But sleep isn't so easy to come by when you're expecting an earthquake later on. So instead she stretched across the bed and grabbed a study guide for her high-school entrance exams. At least her time-travelling might help her prepare for that, since she'd already gained an extra day.

Before she knew it, Kazuko had dozed off with the book on her face. Then came a low, thundering sound followed by a violent shaking. It was the earthquake!

"I knew it!" shrieked Kazuko, jumping out of bed and into the hallway, where her sisters and mother were already scurrying around in fear.

"There's no need to be scared!" called Kazuko. "It's not a big earthquake!"

Once Kazuko had managed to calm her sisters and her mother down, she put on her shoes and headed off for Goro's house. The fire from the bathhouse would be starting about now, and if she hurried she might be able to let people know before any serious damage was done. She even thought about shouting *Fire! Fire!* But there was a chance that people might think she was just exaggerating.

Unlike the way she'd remembered it, there was nobody to be seen when she reached the bathhouse. But she could clearly see smoke rising from the edges of the back door as well as the occasional red spark. She thought about shouting out *Fire!* But instead she held her breath. After all, if Goro hadn't believed her story, then it might not look good in his eyes if she were to be the first on the scene. He might think she'd started it herself to make her story seem true. Then she'd be branded an arsonist, and the police would come to take her away. It was a thought that made her body shiver. But what could she do instead? Surely she couldn't just stand there idly and watch the flames spread.

PANIC IN PYJAMAS

At that moment Shin, a young employee from the local rice shop, stepped out of the bathhouse with his bath bag in hand. He'd noticed the smoke and sparks, gathered his things quickly together and come outside to spread the news with his famously loud voice.

"Fire!" he called out. "There's a fire!"

And in an instant, doors and shutters seemed to open everywhere, and people spilt out onto the street.

"Someone call the fire department!"

"They just went to do that."

"Where is the fire?"

"It's in the kitchen in the bathhouse!"

A few minutes later the fire trucks arrived on the scene, followed by the police, who immediately began herding the onlookers.

"Kazuko!" came Goro's voice through the crowds. "You were right. Your prediction came true!" he said, running towards her with an unusually pale face.

"So Kazuko was right after all," said Kazuo, who seemed to have appeared out of nowhere and was now standing behind her with a similarly pale face.

"Kazuo!" said Kazuko, turning to see her friend. "Wait a minute. I thought you said you didn't own any pyjamas!"

"Well I didn't then," answered Kazuo. "I used to just sleep in my underwear. But when I got home my mother had bought me these ones."

"So Kazuko really does have the power to predict the future!" said Goro with a hint of admiration.

"Not predicting the future," said Kazuko. "It's something stranger than that."

"What do you mean?" said Goro.

"I'm not predicting the future. I'm jumping back through time. But I can never be sure when it might happen. And if I jump back again, I'm going to have to convince you both all over again."

"You don't have to worry about that any more," said Goro, shaking his head vigorously with his eyes wide-open. "I already believe in your powers."

Kazuo burst out laughing. "But if this was today or yesterday afternoon, you wouldn't have believed it. No matter how much she explained."

Goro made a sour face.

"Well, yeah… I guess you're right…"

Although Kazuko found Goro's confusion amusing, she didn't feel like laughing.

"This is horrible," she said. "There must be some way for things to become normal again!"

"But that special power…" said Goro, turning to Kazuo. "What's it called again?"

"Teleportation," said Kazuo, in a matter-of-fact tone.

"Yes, teleportation. That's a special power!"

"That's true, Goro," replied Kazuko. "But I don't like the fact that I'm the only person who seems to have this power. Even you are looking at me differently now because of it – like you don't think I'm human any more."

"Now you're just being paranoid," said Kazuo, smiling.

"But I'm right, aren't I? Once people find out about this, nobody will ever treat me like a normal person again!"

"Now hold on a minute!" said Kazuo, trying to calm the situation. "We still don't know if you really do have such powers. I mean, you've only gone back in time once, right? It could have been a random and isolated happening. Or maybe you did have a special power, but now you've used it all up in one go!"

"You could be right, I guess. But I still feel uncomfortable not knowing whether it could happen again at any moment."

As the last of the flames were extinguished and the last of the onlookers turned and made their way home, Kazuko and her two friends decided it would be better to talk about everything in the morning, so they went back home to bed. Kazuko tried hard to fall asleep, but her mind was racing with questions. Should she confide in a teacher? And if so, which teacher? Would any of them take her seriously? Or would they just laugh? Eventually her mind grew tired, and she dozed off without noticing. And when she awoke, the morning light was streaming into the room casting lacy patterns on the floor. *Oh no!* she thought to herself as she scrambled out of bed. *Today is Wednesday the nineteenth! The day she and Goro were nearly hit by a truck! Why didn't I think to warn Goro last night! How could I forget until now!*

Looking at the clock, she decided there was still time to do something. So she threw on her clothes, gulped down her breakfast and sprinted out of the house.

When she arrived at the zebra crossing, Kazuko let out a sigh of relief. Goro hadn't arrived yet, so she could stand there and wait for him. But it wasn't going to be that simple. As she stood there even for a few moments, she could see her classmates passing her, wondering why she wasn't heading for school too. And what if anyone asked her? What would she say she was doing? She couldn't tell them she was waiting to save Goro from being flattened by a speeding truck. They'd think she'd done too much studying for her entrance exams and driven herself crazy in the process.

A few moments later, Mariko came along.

"Oh, Kazuko. Why are you standing here?"

Here we go! thought Kazuko to herself. "I'm waiting for Goro."

As an explanation it was innocent enough. But Mariko chose to read a little more into it. Maybe it was because she'd always been a little jealous of Kazuko's friendship with him and Kazuo.

"Ooh, waiting for Goro, are you?" said Mariko with a cheeky smile spreading across her face. "That's interesting. I always thought you liked Kazuo more."

"Don't be ridiculous!" said Kazuko, blushing. "It's not like that at all."

"It's okay." Mariko let out a high-pitched laugh and patted Kazuko on the shoulder. "There's no need to hide your feelings. But you know Goro is always late. Careful you aren't late too!"

Kazuko stomped in frustration as Mariko stepped out onto the zebra crossing. Then, just as the traffic light turned red, along came Goro dashing around the corner.

"Morning!" he said in between deep breaths. "Looks like we're both running late, huh?"

I'm only running late because I was waiting for you! thought Kazuko to herself. There was no point in complaining to Goro now. The most important thing right now was for her make sure Goro stayed off the road until the traffic light turned green again.

"You know, most accidents happen when someone is running late," said Kazuko.

"Don't say that. You'll put a jinx on us."

"But it's a fact."

"Well, we don't need your facts or your worrying maternal instincts right now, thank you."

"Fair enough. Just don't go jumping out into the street the moment the lights change."

"Okay, okay!"

A few seconds later, the light changed, and Goro made an exaggerated look to the left and right before getting ready to step out.

"Wait!" screamed Kazuko.

Surely enough, a large truck was hurtling towards them from the other side of the intersection, and Goro jumped back in panic.

"Wow! What's up with that truck!" said Goro incredulously, and the two of them stood transfixed as the truck careered past them and mounted the pavement, causing the screams of terrified pedestrians to fill the air.

From the crowd, a voice called out, "The driver's asleep!"

Then, just a moment later, the truck slammed into a large trash bin on the street, sending it flying into a man walking nearby and knocking him to the ground. From there, the truck continued, sending a young housewife flying too, before finally smashing into the front of a store selling western clothes – hurling shards of broken glass in all directions. Once it came to a stop, Kazuko could see that the windscreen was broken, the front half of the truck was twisted beyond repair, and smoke was beginning to rise from the engine.

"Help!" Came a shout, as a middle-aged man came limping out of the shop – his clothes covered in blood and his face frozen in shock. Then came another voice – the scream of a woman from inside the shop. And as all of this unfolded before their eyes, Kazuko and Goro could do nothing but stand and watch.

THE CONSULTATION

Following the crash, the intersection descended into chaos. People from all over the neighbourhood were rushing to the scene, and the piercing sound of police and ambulance sirens grew louder and louder. More onlookers seemed to come from out of nowhere, and Kazuko and Goro remained where they stood in a daze.

Goro turned to Kazuko, his eyes wide with amazement. "So many weird things happen when you're around."

"How dare you say that!"

"What? Don't get hysterical because of what just happened!"

"You don't even know what just happened!"

Since Kazuko and Goro were now very late for class, they stopped their bickering and started to walk quickly. And as they went, Kazuko explained everything to Goro.

"So if I hadn't hung around waiting for you. If I hadn't stopped you, then both of us could have been—"

"Hit by that truck!" said Goro, jumping in to complete her sentence as a shiver ran down his spine.

"That's right."

When they eventually got to school, class had already begun.

"Ah, late together, eh?" said Mr Fukushima as the two of them walked sheepishly into the room, causing all their classmates to laugh. But when he saw how pale they both looked, he decided to stop teasing them and get back to teaching.

Goro and Kazuko quietly took their seats, but since their hearts were still racing they were in no mind to concentrate on their studies.

That's it! thought Kazuko as she glared at the blackboard, *I can ask Mr Fukushima about it. He's been teaching me since the first year, he's kind and he's a science teacher, which could be handy for a problem like this. I'll ask Goro and Kazuo to come with me and ask him.*

Kazuko discussed the idea with her friends at break time and in the hallway between classes, attracting eyebrows raised in curiosity from Mariko and some of their other classmates. Then, after the day's classes had finished, they nervously went to knock on the door of the staff room – hoping they could catch him out of earshot of the other teachers. Luckily, they found him sitting alone in the corner, so they crowded around him for a private discussion, with Kazuko speaking first.

"Mr Fukushima?"

Their teacher looked up in surprise and put down his science magazine.

"Ah, it's you lot," he said, cracking his characteristic smile. "Have you come to apologize for being late this morning?"

"Well, it does have something to do with being late," said Kazuko. "But I also want to ask your advice."

"Is that right? Well, take a seat." Mr Fukushima casually dragged three chairs over and invited them to sit, then he lit a cigarette. "So, what's this all about?"

Kazuo was the best at speaking, and his friends had agreed he should speak first. "Well first of all, it's important for us to ask you to hear us out to the end without laughing. I say that because any normal person may well think our story sounds stupid or like a dream or make-believe, and so most people might just shrug it off. We weren't even sure if we should tell anyone at all, but in the end we decided you might understand."

"I see," said Mr Fukushima, the smile disappearing from his face. "Seems like a complicated situation."

"That's right."

"And you've come to me in confidence. Right. I will listen to the end without laughing."

"Thank you," said Kazuo with a relieved expression. "It's actually about Kazuko here…" And so Kazuo began telling Kazuko's incredible story.

A LEAP IN TIME

When Kazuo finished his long monologue about what happened to Kazuko, Mr Fukushima heaved a sigh and remained lost in thought.

"Hmm. I see," he said quietly.

Kazuko watched Mr Fukushima's every move with pleading eyes and felt extremely impatient. *Please believe us!* she pleaded in her mind. *If you don't, there's no one else we can turn to!*

Goro couldn't stand the silence any longer. "So Mr Fukushima, do you believe us?" he blurted out, his voice betraying his urgency.

Mr Fukushima looked at each of them slowly, then nodded slightly.

"Of course. I will believe you. I don't think you three would go to the trouble of telling such a lie as a prank – and, besides, I can tell that something shocking has happened to Kazuko just by looking at your faces."

Already, Kazuo and Goro began to feel a little relieved. As for Kazuko, she could hardly contain her happiness at the thought that Mr Fukushima was on their side.

"By the way, Kazuko," Mr Fukushima said, his eyes unfocused as though he were still lost in thought. "Since this has started happening to you, or even before it started happening, how is your health?"

"Well I'm glad you asked. I actually don't feel quite the same as before. I can't explain it well, but I have this 'floating' feeling."

"When did this start?"

"It started, I think, on that Saturday after classes, when I smelt that chemical in the science lab."

Mr Fukushima brought his hand down on the desk.

"Ah, I remember that. That was the time you said you saw someone suspicious?"

"Yes."

"Wait, so that makes it four days ago…"

Mr Fukushima wrote down the date in his notebook and went back to his thoughts.

"Mr Fukushima, do such mysterious things happen from time to time?" Goro asked timidly. "Even though it's happening right in front of my eyes, I'm still having trouble believing it. Is this something that happens often?"

Mr Fukushima nodded slowly.

"It's no surprise you're having trouble. Anyone would. Any ordinary person – when faced with such a mysterious set of events, things that can't be explained by science as we know it – would be so bewildered that they would rather forget about it quickly without investigating properly. Our instincts tell us to fear this kind of phenomenon. Goro, I assume you are no exception?"

Goro hesitated a little before vaguely nodding. "Yeah, well, I guess…"

"But science is a discipline that gives us the tools to analyse things that are mysterious and discover the facts that make them normal. So for us to make discoveries, we must first be faced with mysteries. No mysteries, no new discoveries!" added Mr Fukushima with a sparkle in his eye.

Kazuko had never seen Mr Fukushima like this. Kazuo and Goro were also drawn in by the passion with which he was speaking, and were listening closely.

"So, incidents like the one experienced by Kazuko could be happening more often than we think. Indeed there are similar occurrences reported from all around the world. There are people who collect these stories and are investigating them. For example, Francis Edwards is one of them, but because he's a researcher and not really a scientist, he simply records such facts."

"But how would you explain what's happened to Kazuko?" Kazuo asked.

"I would say, teleportation and time leap."

"Time leap?"

"Yup. They are not as clear as in Kazuko's case, but there are similar phenomena happening around the world. For example on 23rd September 1880, on a farm near Gallatin in Texas, a man named David Lang vanished in front of his wife, two kids and two friends. Simply disappeared while five people were watching. Also, in a small area off the south-east coast of the US, over twenty airplanes have mysteriously vanished. In these cases, the ones who disappeared haven't been found, and the theory is that they leapt through time and ended up far in the future or far in the past. As an example of teleportation, there was a case of a person who one day disappeared from Tokyo and reappeared around the same time in Kimberley, USA. There are many stories like this from way back."

RETURN TO FOUR DAYS AGO

Kazuko and her friends were awestruck. They'd never heard such stories in their lives.

"So in my case both teleportation and time leap happened simultaneously," said Kazuko.

"That's the only plausible explanation," nodded Mr Fukushima. "When the truck was about to hit you, in addition to thinking of yourself in bed, you were also wishing to be far away in terms of time. That's why you leapt through time to a place way before the incident."

"But why was I able to—"

"Do such a thing? Well, that's the thing," said Mr Fukushima, jotting more things down in his notebook. "I think it was triggered by that chemical you smelt in the science lab four days ago. If I remember correctly, you fainted after smelling that lavender-scented chemical?"

"Yes, that's right."

"The problem is that chemical. That chemical probably gave you these powers. By the way, don't you like having this power?"

"No, I don't!" blurted Kazuko. "I don't like being the only one with powers."

"I understand. And that's a normal reaction. You don't want others thinking you're not a normal human, right? I understand how you feel. But what you need to do now is to use this power of yours to return to that science lab four days ago when this incident started."

"What! Why?... And how?"

All three of them were surprised by his suggestion.

"By leaping through time, of course!" said Mr Fukushima, sounding even more surprised than Kazuko. "I mean, you have the powers, and you've already done it once, right?"

"But I was terrified of being hit by that truck and…"

Mr Fukushima raised his hand and stopped her.

"I know. And by looking into what psychological and physical state you were in at the time, we should be able to recreate the same conditions."

"But Mr Fukushima, even if Kazuko can leap back in time by four days, what will she do when she gets there?" asked Kazuo, looking worried.

"She will need to meet that mysterious person who made the chemical," explained Mr Fukushima, beaming at Kazuko. "She will have to get to that person before he or she makes the chemical. I think that will solve the problem. It might be a little risky, but I think Kazuko can do it."

Kazuko fell silent, lost in thought. *That's right!* she thought. *If I can prevent that person from making the chemical, maybe I can make everything go back to normal.*

"The biggest problem here is…" Kazuo said thoughtfully, "how are we going to make Kazuko leap back in time?"

Mr Fukushima reflected on this for a moment. "Kazuko, can you remember what you were thinking and feeling when the truck was about to hit you?"

"I'm afraid not," Kazuko said with a sad expression, shaking her head. "I don't think I'd have any idea unless I was in a similar situation again."

"I totally understand," said Goro, feeling a slight shiver as he remembered the accident in the morning. "And we can't put Kazuko in such a dangerous situation again…"

"Okay. I will think of a way," said Mr Fukushima as he got to his feet.

When they looked around, they realized that all the other teachers had already gone home and the staff room was now empty.

"You guys are going home, right? Should we walk out together?"

The three of them left the school with Mr Fukushima. As they stepped out and walked home along the edge of a building site, the cold wind blew gusts at them as they passed gaps in its large boarding fence.

"If I were to go back four days, would you all be willing to help me?"

"I'd say yes," replied Kazuo, "but I can't promise anything. I didn't know about anything mysterious four days ago. So if you'd told me anything then, I'm afraid I probably wouldn't have believed you."

"And I might be even more sceptical," added Goro.

"So you're saying I need to work out this problem all on my own?"

But before anyone could answer, Mr Fukushima ran off the pavement and shouted, "Run! There's a steel beam falling!"

Only two or three days ago, at this precise location, a piece of lumber had fallen onto the pavement injuring several people. Kazuo and Goro screamed and followed

Mr Fukushima, but Kazuko remained rooted to the spot in terror. *I'm going to be crushed to death!* she thought. And the moment that thought came to her mind, a strange feeling engulfed her.

ALONE IN THE CITY AT NIGHT

Kazuko felt her body lift lightly in the air, as if picked up by some large invisible being. *I need to move!* she thought. *Got to get away before I'm crushed!*

It was almost as if her sheer need to be somewhere else had actually made her body become weightless. What's more, Kazuko's vision suddenly darkened, her ears rang, and then finally... there was silence.

When Kazuko regained consciousness, it was already midnight. Stars sparkled in the night sky. But only a little while earlier, she remembered seeing the late afternoon sun as it tinged the buildings a blushing red.

"Mr Fukushima!" called out Kazuko. She was about to call for Kazuo and Goro too, but instead she noticed that she was now all alone. She was standing on the road, right where she'd wanted to be to escape the falling beam. But when she turned back to the pavement, the beam was nowhere to be seen.

Kazuko gasped and covered her face with both hands. She glanced along the road that had been teeming with traffic and pedestrians just moments earlier, but there were no cars and no people any more. So it really was late after all, and she really was all alone – just Kazuko on a dreary street corner at midnight. Then it all started to make sense to her. *A-ha!* she thought. *I must have leapt through time. That would explain everything!*

As she stood there clutching her bag in the freezing night air, she wondered if there had even been a falling beam at all. Perhaps Mr Fukushima had just said that to see if it would make her time-leap. If that was his plan, then it must have worked. But how far in time had she leapt? What time was it now? Was it a different day? Or had she gone back more than a day?

Kazuko thought hard for several minutes, then she had an idea. She pulled out the notebook she always used in class and wondered if it might answer her questions. As she flipped through the pages, she noticed that all the notes she'd taken that day were already gone, and so were her notes from yesterday, which meant that she had travelled back two days to either the night of Monday the seventeenth or the early morning on Tuesday the eighteenth. Judging by the biting cold of the air, Kazuko felt pretty sure it was early on Tuesday morning.

In that case, I should be fast asleep in my bed at this very moment, thought Kazuko. *But then,* she thought, *I'm standing here. So if I'm here now, does that mean there's another me asleep in my bed?*

Kazuko shook her head vigorously. So many unbelievable things had happened to her since just the other day that it was difficult to take everything in. And if there was another Kazuko asleep at her house right now, then where should the time-leaping Kazuko go? It was all so very confusing, and Kazuko hadn't a clue what to do. If she tried to stay out all night, then surely she'd freeze to death. Or what if a patrolling policeman came across her? He'd think she was a runaway, and probably insist on taking her to the station. So what on earth should she do? Without making any clear decision, Kazuko simply started wandering in the direction of her house.

I could at least try going home, she thought to herself. *Maybe I could peek through the window first. It would be extremely scary, of course, to see myself asleep in my own bed. But I have to know!*

Kazuko plodded along, shivering, until she arrived at her doorstep. Unsurprisingly, the front door was locked, so she opened the gate at the side of the house and made her way to the back instead. Quietly and carefully, she approached her window, worrying all the while that someone might see her and think she was a burglar. But luckily, there were no policemen around and no dogs to bark at her either. So, slowly, she pressed her face against the glass and peered into her room, looking first to her night-light, that lent a comforting glow to the room, and then slowly trailing her eyes to the bed.

A JOURNEY BEYOND YESTERDAY

When she saw that there was nobody in her bed, Kazuko let out a big sigh of relief. But on the other hand, the bed did look quite untidy – as if someone had been sleeping in it just moments earlier. As her relief subsided, she realized that she had yet another problem to deal with. Her window was locked from the inside, as was the front door and the door to the kitchen, so there was no way for her to get back inside the house. She'd always felt safe, knowing her mother was so cautious. But now that she was standing on the other side, the feeling was quite different.

But what should I do? she thought to herself. *I can't possibly ring the doorbell at this hour and have my mother come to the door. After all, I was supposed to be in bed hours ago!*

By now, Kazuko's legs were shaking, and her teeth were chattering. Inside the house, her room looked so cosy and warm, with a plume of steam coming from a little kettle placed on top of the heater and the windows fogging with condensation inside. *If I don't get inside soon,* she thought, *I'm going to freeze to death out here!*

At that very moment, Kazuko felt her body lift in the air. It was the same strange feeling she'd felt earlier at the construction site, only this time she'd made it happen herself. With her own will. Her own power of thought. *I did it!* she thought. *I'm about to leap!*

As the strange floating sensation grew stronger, Kazuko did her best to keep her mind focused on the inside of her room. Then suddenly, just like before, everything went dark and her ears began to ring.

The very next moment, Kazuko saw a bright light that somehow made her feel dizzy. Then, as the intensity of the light faded, she found herself standing inside her room in the bright afternoon sunlight.

"It's the afternoon!" Kazuko yelped in surprise. "And I can time-leap! All by myself! Without anyone's help!"

Having yelled all that out of sheer happiness, Kazuko came to her senses and covered her mouth.

How stupid am I? she thought. *It would be a disaster if Mother heard me! Besides, I don't even know what time of day it is right now! I don't even know if it's morning*

*or afternoon... or if I'm still supposed to be at school...
Mother will be so mad at me!*

Kazuko stopped panicking and listened carefully.
There was not a sound in the house, so maybe Kazuko's
mother and younger sisters were all out. Or had she leapt
to yet a different day again? Quickly, she reached once
more inside her bag for her notebook. But when she
opened it, she saw there were no new notes since Friday
the fourteenth, and all the pages after that were blank.

So that means it's now Friday afternoon, thought Kazuko to herself. *That means I jumped three days into the
past this time. But can I really assume it's Friday? It could
even be Saturday. After all, I'm here at home now, so I
might have missed my Saturday morning class.*

"Oh my gosh," said Kazuko to herself. "How can I
figure this out?"

She glanced around the room, but there was no clock
and no calendar to give her a clue, so instead she sneaked
out into the hallway. *Please be empty!* she prayed to
herself as she approached the living room.

As slowly and carefully as she could, Kazuko slid
open the wooden door with its panels made of paper.
Luckily there was nobody there. But there was a clock
showing the time as 10:30.

10:30 a.m.! she thought. *That's in the middle of the third period!* And with not a moment to lose, she dashed back to her room and grabbed her bag. It was Saturday morning after all, and she simply had to get to school! Because it wasn't just any Saturday morning. This was the Saturday on which she'd stayed behind after class. The same Saturday when she'd caught a glimpse of that mysterious figure and all this mess had begun. So she had to make sure she was back in the science lab at the right moment and face that person before he or she could disappear again.

BACK TO THE LAB

Kazuko arrived at school during the ten-minute break between the third and fourth periods. She felt slightly relieved: if she was careful, she wouldn't have to explain her absence to the teacher. She might just be able to walk back in with the other students and act as if nothing had happened. But the moment she walked back in with her classmates, her plan fell to pieces.

All of a sudden, her classmates ran to gather around her with surprised faces.

"Kazuko!" said Mariko. "Where have you been?"

"What do you mean, where?" Kazuko asked.

Mariko's voice turned into a high-pitched screech. "This is no time for kidding around! You just disappeared, right in the middle of the third period!"

"Disappeared?"

"That's right," added Goro, who was standing at her side. "You sneaking out like that got everyone worried. I mean, no one even saw you leave the room. Even the teacher up front didn't see you stand up, and no one heard the door open."

"That's right," Mariko screeched again. "Even I didn't notice you leave, and I was sitting next to you!"

Kazuo, with his usual dazed look, also joined the conversation.

"It's almost as if Kazuko used magic! You disappeared, just like smoke!"

Kazuko struggled to piece together what it could all mean. She'd wondered earlier on if there might be a problem of there being two Kazukos if she jumped back in time. So perhaps what they were talking about explained how the problem gets resolved. Could it be that every leap back in time triggers the disappearance of herself from that particular present time? That would explain why the Kazuko everyone was worrying about had disappeared at probably the same moment the future Kazuko had appeared back in her bedroom. But how on earth was she going to explain that to her friends? It wasn't until days later that she explained everything to them, so there was no way she could expect them to believe her at this moment.

"So, where were you?" Mariko shrieked hysterically

yet again, frustrated that something so strange could happen right next to her without her even noticing.

"I didn't feel well, so I went to the bathroom," offered Kazuko.

"To the bathroom? With your bag?" Mariko wasn't having any of it, and her eyes remained fixed on Kazuko's bag, which she was clutching tightly to her chest.

Fortunately at that moment the teacher, Mr Komatsu, entered the room and all the students immediately stopped talking and dashed back to their seats. Kazuko also took her seat and got out her textbook and notebook from her bag – ready to take notes from a class that she'd already sat through once in the past.

By the time the class was over, Kazuko was very relieved to find that her classmates had pretty much lost interest in questioning her about her disappearance. Then, just like before, Kazuko was asked by Mr Fukushima to clean the science lab with Goro and Kazuo.

By the time they finished cleaning, the school had emptied out, and all was silent apart from the occasional sound of a door slamming shut here and there and the distant sound of someone playing Chopin's 'Polonaise' on the piano in the auditorium.

"That's good enough," said Kazuko. "I'll take out the trash. You boys can go wash your hands."

"Okay. Thanks."

Kazuo and Goro left for the lavatories together, and as soon as they were gone, Kazuko went into the small science lab.

Goro and Kazuo were washing their hands in the sink, talking.

"Kazuko's cute, and she's nice, too. But she can be a little overbearing at times, can't she."

"Oh yeah?" said Kazuo, who had been miles away again. "What makes you say that?"

"Don't you think she can be overbearing?" said Goro, puffing up his chest to match his face, which was always rather red and puffy. "She treats us like we're kids. Come on. *You boys can go and wash your hands*, she says."

Meanwhile, Kazuko was hiding behind the partition in the science lab, waiting for the mysterious person to arrive. Her heart was pounding.

It's nearly time! she thought. *I need to hold my ground!* Kazuko puffed up her chest and flexed the muscles in her arms and legs. Just then, the door to the science lab opened, and someone stepped in slowly.

This is him... thought Kazuko.

IDENTIFYING THE INTRUDER

Kazuko thought she would be able to remain out of the enemy's sight for a while. But maybe she was being a bit hasty by thinking of him as the enemy. After all, she had no reason to believe that he meant her any harm. Come to think of it, she had no reason to believe it was a he! It could just as easily be a girl! But whoever it was, that person had caused a lot of difficulty for Kazuko, and she was determined to get to the bottom of it.

Only moments later, the shadowy figure walked over to the chemicals cabinet, where he or she began rummaging through its contents. Kazuko then heard the clatter of chemical bottles and test tubes being lined up on the desk.

If I can just stay out of sight a little longer, thought Kazuko, *that person will begin making the strange chemical concoction again. Then I'll step out of the shadows and catch the intruder red-handed!*

But in reality, Kazuko was too scared to do anything like that. What if that person was violent? What if that person decided to attack her to protect his or her secret? After all, she was only a girl. What hope did she have of protecting herself? If only she'd asked one of her friends to accompany her... But it was too late. And what was the point – she knew they wouldn't have believed her anyway! There was no choice. She'd simply have to face the intruder by herself. But what sort of a person could it be? She knew that the intruder was capable of giving her superhuman powers. So was that person a genius? A lunatic? Or even a monster? She didn't like her new-found powers, and she really didn't want her friends to think she was any different to anybody else. So she needed to look this person in the face and demand that she be made normal again. And if that didn't work, then maybe she'd have to trick or threaten that person into making her normal again But what would she do if the intruder didn't want to or was unable to do what she wanted? What would she do then! Kazuko began to worry.

Getting a grip on herself, Kazuko remained silent and listened to the sound of chemicals being mixed.

This is the moment to make my move! she thought to herself. But her legs felt like jelly, and she couldn't get them to work. *What am I waiting for! I've gone through so much trouble to be here, and if I don't do something, then it will all have been for nothing!*

You're a coward, Kazuko!

Then suddenly there came a voice: "Okay, Kazuko. You can come out now. I've known all along that you were hiding there."

It was a voice Kazuko knew well. The voice of someone close to her. Surely, it couldn't be him!

Kazuko gingerly stepped away from the partition to find the intruder standing by the chemicals cabinet, smiling at her.

"Kazuo!" screamed Kazuko in both surprise and relief as her friend stood before her with his usual daydreaming expression.

Was he really the one she was after? Could it really be that Kazuo – who'd been with her through this whole thing – was the intruder? Kazuko found it hard to believe. But she knew she had to, and that it would be better if she could hear it directly from him.

"So it was you? You made that odd chemical and gave me these strange powers?" said Kazuko, doing her best to suppress her anger. He was supposed to be her friend, but he'd been watching her suffer all along without ever saying a word!

"Yes, that's right. But I didn't do it to cause you trouble. It was just a coincidence that you came to have those powers. I didn't mean for it to happen. There's a reason why I didn't tell you before. I was trying to protect you. I just hope you can believe me!"

"But, but..." Kazuko was suddenly lost for words.

There were so many questions, so many things she wanted to say. "I just can't believe it. Why would you..."

Kazuo wore a smile of pity on his face, and Kazuko was surprised to see there was something a little more mature about him. Not like when some of the students pretend to be grown-ups, but a genuine maturity. The person standing in front of her was no longer a boy – at least not like the rest of the kids at school.

THE BOY FROM THE FUTURE

"I don't know how to tell you this..." Kazuo said thoughtfully. "It's going to take a little time to explain. But believe me when I say everything I'm about to tell you is the truth. And you should now have an easier time believing me because of everything you've been through. To put it simply, Kazuko, I am... from, er, the future."

"From the future?" Kazuko was shocked. She thought she was prepared to hear anything, but this was well beyond her expectations – well beyond common sense, or what she believed was common sense, anyway.

"I... I can't believe it," said Kazuko, her voice trembling.

"I thought you might say that," said Kazuo with a nod. "It's a bit like science fiction, isn't it?"

But Kazuko wasn't in any mood to make light of the situation. "So how did you get here? In some sort of time machine or something?" she asked in a sarcastic voice.

"No. I came just like you did. By time-leaping and teleportation."

As she struggled to take this all in, Kazuko felt a bit faint, and the room started to spin a little.

"If you can't believe what I'm saying, that's okay," continued Kazuo. "You can just listen to it as if it were a fairy tale. You've suffered enough, so you have the right to hear my story. But don't blame me if you think my story is outrageous. I'm not going to lie to you. But it's the only explanation I have."

"All right," said Kazuko. "I'll listen."

"Okay. I'll tell you. But let's stop time before we start. We don't want anyone interrupting us."

"What?" Kazuko yelled.

Unruffled by her shock, Kazuo reached into his pocket and pulled out something that looked like a transistor radio, and extended its antenna.

"Okay. Now we are the only people moving and talking in this world. If you don't believe me, take a look out the window."

Kazuko wondered if Kazuo might be losing his mind.

"Go on!" said Kazuo. "Have a look, if you don't believe me." And with that, he took her hand and led her to the window.

Kazuko allowed herself to be led to the window, noticing at the same time how cold Kazuo's hand was and how much it felt like the hand of a woman. Then, when they reached the window, they both stared out at the road in front of the school.

Kazuko was dumbfounded. There were cars on the road as usual, but not one of them was moving. Buses, trucks and passenger cars – they were all frozen to the spot. Even more amazingly, Kazuko could see people on the pavement and the zebra crossing arrested in midstep. There was even a dog that must have been sprinting along, because it was now just hanging in the air with each of its paws a good ten centimetres off the ground!

"Time really has stopped," whispered Kazuko, noticing the silence all around them.

"You could say that," offered Kazuo. "Or, to be more accurate, you could say that we are backtracking at exactly the same speed as time is moving forward. So it's only to our eyes that time appears to be standing still."

"But how can you do such a thing?"

"It's this device. It's releasing a very strong energy field around us, cutting us off from the outside world and moving time backwards inside. It's a barrier with all sorts of applications."

"I don't think I understand…"

"That's fine. You don't really have to understand how it works," said Kazuo casually as he took her hand, and led her back to the middle of the science lab. "Okay then." He continued with a smile. "Let's start from the very beginning."

IN THE YEAR 2660

Kazuo's story went something like this.

Throughout the twenty-seventh century, the Earth's population had been increasing exponentially. There were colonies on both the Moon and Mars, and many people were forced to go there due to the extreme overcrowding back on our planet. At least that was the way it was for people who didn't have so much money or social status. But for the people who did have money and status, they remained on Earth, where they were busy working on the development of a new civilization run by machines.

By the year 2620, the peaceful use of nuclear energy had freed mankind to concentrate on other issues, and many bold new discoveries had been made in much shorter time than ever before. But because science was progressing so fast, the general public began to have difficulties in keeping up with it. In time, the various technologies surpassed the understanding of many scientists as well, who had become more specialized and had to delegate their work. So even though the scientists knew how to do their jobs very well, each of them concentrated only on one small task and they were not abreast of all the other technological developments. In fact, they no longer needed to know much about anything other than the one simple job they'd been allocated. Needless to say, this had a rather bad effect on society.

In the beginning, it was schools and other educational institutions that suffered the most. In the past, they'd been able to teach a range of subjects to students at a basic level. But now such basic information was no use to anybody in such an advanced world. So schooling was extended. Kids were sent to elementary school from the age of four. Then, for fourteen years they were taught basic education. Then junior education followed this for five years, and that concluded compulsory education. Completing compulsory education, however, didn't mean you were ready to take a job. Simple tasks and calculations were performed by machines and computerized brains, so no human with a junior-high-school-level education was much use in any work place. If one wanted to become an office worker, more specialized education was required in a specific field, so you had to attend high school or a specialized school for another five years.

After all that education, graduates were finally fit to become just an average technician or to take a clerical role, but to become a medical doctor or a scientist would require even more training. So by the time one had graduated from an institution as a specialist, that person would already be thirty-eight at the youngest, or in many cases closer to fifty years old. This meant that people didn't really have time to get married until after forty, which finally led to a much-needed decrease in the Earth's population.

"This is a disaster. If we continue down this path we'll go extinct," said those in the future. Kazuo explained that the doctors and scientists got together to try to find a solution. And in 2640, they succeeded in developing a truly revolutionary invention. It was a new kind of educational method called sleep education or subconscious-awareness education.

"What's sleep education?" asked Kazuko, mesmerized. In the beginning, she'd wondered if this was all made up, but it seemed too detailed and realistic to be only a story.

"Sleep education," explained Kazuo, his eyes lighting up with excitement, "is a method in which information and memories are planted directly into a child's brain. A magnetic tape is loaded with information, connected to the child's head with electrodes and played back. The human unconscious has outstanding capacities, and is able to recall this information whenever it's needed. With this invention, it took a lot less time to educate people. So if this educational method is begun at the age of three, by the time the child is about the equivalent age of a first-year junior-high student they will have finished education through to current university level. I personally have been through this system too, so..." Kazuo's voice trailed off.

"So how old are you now, really?" asked Kazuko.

Kazuo looked a little embarrassed before replying. "I'm eleven."

"What!?" Dumbfounded, Kazuko looked at Kazuo, who was at least ten centimetres taller than her. "But that makes you four years younger than me! Is that true?"

Kazuo scratched his head and smiled. "The thing is, in 2660, children simply develop faster. So from my point of view, of course, the children in this time are suffering from growth deficiency."

"So you're saying we're underdeveloped?" said Ka-zuko, sounding a little annoyed.

"Don't get angry. In 2660, all foods are super-nutritious. That's how we maintain the balance between spirit and body. You understand, right? If we don't maintain a kind of balance, we could end up with super-educated babies, and that would just be creepy, wouldn't it?"

"Are you telling me that you have university-level academic ability?"

Kazuo nodded. "That's right. I'm at university studying pharmaceutical science."

No wonder he was a good student, thought Kazuko.

"But why did you come to this moment in time? And to this school? And why are you pretending to be someone from my time attending school? Don't you want to go back to the future?"

Kazuo tried to stop the flood of questions thrown at him by Kazuko. "Wait, wait. Let me explain one thing at a time."

AN UNEXPECTED CONFESSION

Kazuo was born in 2649. Just like the other children he spoke about, he was educated with the sleep tapes from the age of three and entered university to study pharmaceuticals at the age of eleven. Right around that time, a great number of new chemicals were being developed, some of them designed to stimulate and bring out latent abilities in humans. It had already been scientifically proved that humans could develop physical, telekinetic and psychological powers, and so the last challenge remaining for scientists was to find a way to fulfil such potential.

At university, Kazuo was involved in research relating to teleportation by free will. He'd been limited by his university to carry out experiments only at a safe level, but being as bright as he was, Kazuo soon began formulating a whole range of new experiments. One of the areas he'd started to work on was the combination of teleportation and time-leaping, or to put it more simply, the ability to transport oneself instantly to another place and another time. Kazuo felt sure this could be done. He knew that the stimulants for teleportation had already been developed, and that time travel was already possible. All he needed to do was to find a way to incorporate all such capabilities in one stimulant.

After considerable experimentation, Kazuo found that by adding essence of lavender to the stimulant used for teleportation – known as Crox Zilvius – he could achieve the desired effect. And after many more trials and errors, he finally managed to blend exactly the chemical he needed.

All he needed to do then was to run an experiment to test the effect, which he decided to do himself in secret.

"That experiment was a big failure," said Kazuo, scratching his head and laughing.

"You could leap across time. But when you wanted to leap back, you couldn't. Is that right?" asked Kazuko.

"That's right," nodded Kazuo. "I didn't know how effective the potion was going to be, so I drank a small amount. I was able to come here, into the past, but the potion was too weak to get me back to the future."

"You should have brought the potion with you."

"Yeah. I did think of that, and had it ready, but I forgot to bring it."

"For someone so advanced, it's quite surprising to see you still have a scatterbrain side."

"That's not it," answered Kazuo with reddened cheeks. "I was thinking about which time to travel to, since I wanted a fairly peaceful time. But as soon as I thought of one, my mind initiated the time leap and I wasn't holding the stimulant at the time."

"So that's why you became a student of this school, and that's why you sneaked into the science lab?"

"That's right. But then you walked in, surprised me and made me knock it over! Luckily, you didn't drink the stimulant. But you did smell it, so it gave you powers to teleport and to time-leap, but in a limited manner."

"Does that mean my powers will fade away with time?"

"That's right, so you don't have to worry so much."

Kazuko was relieved. "So were you able to make the potion again?"

"Yes, I was." Kazuo pointed at the bottle on the table, filled with brown, steaming liquid.

"But why are you explaining all of this to me?" asked Kazuko.

Kazuo thought carefully for a few moments before answering.

"Well, you seemed to be having such a hard time with the situation, so I felt that I owed you an explanation."

"But from your point of view, I'm someone in the past. If you return to the future there will be no connection between us…"

Kazuo started to look rather sheepish, and his eyes dropped to the ground. Then he took a breath and glanced up to meet her eyes.

"Well, there's a little more to the story than that," he said. "You see, Kazuko, I've… I've fallen in love with you."

PEOPLE OF TOMORROW, PEOPLE OF TODAY

"I guess confessing their love is not such a big thing for people in the future, huh?" said Kazuko, playfully. She knew he was a university student, but the fact that she was older than him in years gave her the confidence to make a joke.

"So do you like older girls?" she quipped.

"That's right, I guess in a sense you are older," said Kazuo, who hadn't thought about that until now.

"Oh you guess, do you?" said Kazuko, a little offended. "Well, I am older. I may be just a person from the past in your eyes who is both physically and mentally underdeveloped, but I can't help that, and yes, I am older."

"That's not what I meant, Kazuko," pleaded Kazuo. "I just don't think of you as being older, that's all. Maybe it's because, I don't know how to explain it, but it could be because we've been studying for a while in the same class together, having fun times together – you, Goro and me.

So I feel very close to you now. Like I've known you for a lot longer. That's why I'm guessing I fell in love with you."

Kazuko felt her cheeks flush a little. No one had ever said out right that they loved her like this. He was just so direct, and Kazuko wondered if perhaps everybody would be like that in the future. For Kazuko, however, love was something quite new. She'd read about it in romantic novels, and there had been playground gossip about other kids falling in love. But it was always something people were teased about – as if it were something to be ashamed of. She'd felt such uncomfortable feelings when Mariko had teased her about liking Goro. But then, Kazuko had always felt that the boys her age were so immature, so she couldn't really imagine having any romantic feelings for them. But now Kazuo was confessing his feelings for her, and it wasn't a joke. It had thrown her completely off balance, and she didn't know what to say. So instead she just stayed silent and kept her eyes fixed on the ground.

"It's like you've known me for a lot longer," said Kazuko to herself, in a daze.

"That's right. That's how I feel," Kazuo said, smiling. "But the time we actually spent together was just a month."

"Just a month?" Kazuko looked up in surprise and shook her head vigorously. "That can't be! We've known each other for a really long time. It's been... two years. Even before that, we weren't really on talking terms, but I've known you since elementary school. I mean, we live in the same neighbourhood!"

"Ah, of course. I forgot to tell you."

"Forgot to tell me what?"

"I gave you, or rather everyone around me, false memories about myself."

"False memories?" Kazuko didn't understand.

"Yes. I actually arrived here about a month ago. But to be able to fit in here comfortably, I had to make it seem as if I'd been here for a long time. So I made a false history about myself and gave it to a lot of people as memory."

"Unbelievable! So you gave those memories to me, to Goro, Mr Fukushima, to Mariko..."

"Yes. Everyone in our class and all the other people who should know me."

"But how were you able to do such a thing?"

"It's not as difficult as you might think. You know about hypnosis, right? If you get someone under hypnosis and tell them they're a bird, they will actually believe that. What I did was similar to that, although the technology involved is much more advanced. Plus, hypnosis is easier to achieve with a big group rather than just one person. It works like a sort of chain reaction, with one person's belief rapidly spreading to the next and so on."

Kazuko had heard something like this from Mr Fukushima. "Group Hypnosis…"

"Right. I did something similar to what you're describing. In my experience the people of this time are extremely prone to hypnosis."

Well, I guess people of my time are all nothing more than barbarians to you! thought Kazuko to herself.

"So that's how I started my life here – as someone who'd been around for a while. I made it so that I was already a student here who had been living in that house for a long time…"

"That house!" Kazuko suddenly thought of Kazuo's parents. "So the people in that house – does that mean they're not your real family?"

"No. They didn't have any kids. So I created a memory that I was their child. They are very good people, and they like plants too. That's one of the reasons I chose them as my host family – because they have plenty of lavenders in their greenhouse. I was going to use them to make Crox Zilvius and then return home. And then, today, I finally finished making the stimulant!"

"So if they're not your real family, I guess that means your name isn't really Kazuo Fukamachi, is it?"

"No. Kazuo Fukamachi is a name I gave myself for living in this time. I have a different name in the future."

"And what's that?"

"My name is…" Kazuo fell silent. "It will probably sound odd to you. But my real name is Ken Sogol."

"Ken Sogol?" Kazuo repeated the name a few times to herself. "It's a nice name."

"Thank you."

"But why didn't you tell me all this sooner? You saw me suffering…"

"Well, when you fainted after smelling the potion, I thought I might be able to just let time take care of it without you ever having to know. You're such a peaceful girl, and I didn't want to ruin your life with such complex and confusing things. But then, unexpectedly, you got into that road accident and you managed to teleport and time-leap. Then you started leaping into the past of your own accord, so that you could meet me! Things had already got so complicated for you, so I decided to travel back in time as well to talk to you."

Well, I guess that answers everything now, thought Kazuko. But Kazuo kept on talking.

"But there is something very important, Kazuko. I'm not actually allowed to tell you any of this. None of us from the future are allowed to talk about this stuff with people from the past."

"But why?"

"Because it confuses history. It has a bad effect on society as well. You can see that, right? If I told people now that a few years down the road they were going to be at war it would cause panic. Especially because there is nothing you can do about it."

"We could prevent the war."

"It doesn't work like that. History often cannot be changed. But if you could change anything, there are plenty of people who would love to take advantage of that for their own profit."

"So there's a law in your own time that says you cannot tell people in the past about the future."

"Yes. That's about right."

"Does that mean you've broken the law? I mean, you've told me everything."

"There are some exceptions."

"Exceptions?"

Kazuo hesitated for a while, then he sighed and continued.

"Even if I talk about the future to someone, if that person doesn't remember it's okay. That is to say, it's okay if I erase your memory about me."

ERASING MEMORIES

Kazuko's eyes flew open in surprise. "Does that mean you'll be erasing *my* memory before you return to the future?"

Kazuo nodded sadly. "It can't be avoided. It's really sad that you won't remember me after I leave, but I'll be punished in my own time if I don't do it."

"But I don't want to forget!" cried Kazuko, shaking her head violently. She thought of all her memories of fun talks with Kazuo, and her memory of him confessing his love for her – memories she simply couldn't bear to lose. And what about the memory of his face! She wouldn't even be able to remember what he looked like!

"But everything that's happened, it's been so precious," pleaded Kazuko. "I don't want to forget. You can remember me, though, can't you? You can remember me for ever. It's not fair that only I have to forget."

"It's not only you! Don't you see? I'll have to erase the memory of everyone who's known me in this time."

"And when are you returning to the future?"

"Right now."

"So soon…" said Kazuko with a tear in her eye.

"Of course I want to stay as long as possible. I'd much rather stay in this time and live happily among people like yourself and Goro. But I have work to do. I need to finish my research."

Kazuko drooped her head. "Well, you are from the future, so I guess I shouldn't be surprised that you should want to return."

"But I do like your time better than the future," said Kazuo without hesitation. "The pace of life is slower here, people are nicer. It's just much easier to live here and to get along with everyone. And, of course, you're here." Kazuo looked into Kazuko's eyes. "Of course, Goro is a great friend, and Mr Fukushima is a great teacher. But if it comes to choosing between staying here and going back to my research, then I have to go back to my research. It is, after all, my main purpose in life."

"But please, don't erase my memory!" begged Kazuko with all her heart. "I won't tell anyone! I promise. I'll keep the memory of you hidden in my heart. I can't stand the thought of losing all my memories of you. I can't!"

Kazuo looked distraught at hearing her words. "I can't do that. Please understand," he said in a low and determined voice.

Realizing her cheeks were wet with tears, Kazuko hurriedly took out her handkerchief and wiped her eyes. Suddenly, she felt rather ashamed at being so emotional in front of Kazuo.

"I understand..." she mumbled. But her heart was too heavy for her to say much more. "So I guess this is it."

Kazuko stood up and took a good look at Kazuo's face, that lovely face that she would surely never see again.

"Are you going now... right now?" she asked.

Kazuo nodded solemnly.

"Can you just tell me one thing?" said Kazuko, her voice cracking. "Are you never going to return to this time? Are you never going to appear in front of me again?"

"I will probably come again. Some day..." said Kazuo as he picked up the radio-like device from the desk and pushed in the antenna.

"But when will that be?"

"I don't know when. Probably when I finish my research, when I succeed in making the potion."

Hearing noises from the road outside, Kazuko realized that time was moving once more.

"So will you come back to see me?" She pleaded again.

Already, Kazuo was starting to fade before her eyes, and she had to struggle to keep him in sight. She watched as a white steam enveloped Kazuo and a strong scent of lavender filled the air.

"I will come to see you, Kazuko," he said, rapidly fading. "Not as Kazuo Fukamachi, but as someone completely new to you."

"I'll know," said Kazuko, struggling to hold on to her consciousness. "I'll know who you are."

Then everything around her went black, and all her strength left her body. And in that brief moment before her body hit the floor, she heard a distant voice.

"Goodbye, Kazuko. Goodbye."

A TIME TO CONNECT

"Come on Kazuko, let's go," came Goro's booming voice as he walked into the science lab. "I've got your bag here!"

"Kazuko!" he shrieked, seeing her lying motionless on the floor. Immediately, he ran over to her and tried to lift her. But she was too heavy for him to lift by himself.

"What should I do!" He said to himself as his eyes welled up with tears. "Maybe you're just exhausted, Kazuko! This lab is far too big for the *two* of us to clean!" And with that, he got up and ran to the staff room for help.

When he got there, he was relieved to see Mr Fukushima sitting there reading, and together they went to the science lab and carried Kazuko back to the nurse's room, where they laid her on the bed and waited for her to wake up.

"Oh. What happened?" she said, with a groggy voice.

"You fainted in the science lab…" said Goro.

Kazuko strained to remember what she was doing in the science lab. But all she could remember was that she'd gone there to put away the brooms.

"Were you the only ones cleaning the science lab?" asked Mr Fukushima.

"That's right," said Goro, puffing out his chest. "Just the two of us cleaning that big room. Me and Kazuko and… That's probably why she fainted, from fatigue."

"I'm sorry to hear that," said Mr Fukushima, sincerely. "I will increase the number of students on the task from tomorrow."

Now that Kazuo had returned to the future, he no longer existed in the hearts of the people of the present. His memory had vanished entirely from the minds of Mr Fukushima, Goro and Kazuko. But more than that, there was simply no Kazuo Fukamachi in this world – with no seat for him in the classroom, nobody noticing his absence, and no reason for anyone to think that anything strange had happened. And when three days had passed, there was also no fire at Goro's house, nobody was late for school, and no truck came careering through the red light at the intersection. Kazuo had seen to it that none of those bad things would happen before he departed for the future and peaceful days returned to Kazuko's life. But every day, on her way home from school, she would pass by a small, nice-looking western-style house where a lovely middle-aged couple lived. Every day, she would pass by the greenhouse next to the house and every day she would enjoy the sweet lavender smell that came from within.

I remember this scent, she would think to herself. *So sweet, so nostalgic. I smelt this somewhere before. But where?*

She could see the name Fukamachi on a shiny name-plate by the door of the house, but it was a name that meant nothing to Kazuko. And at that moment, in her heart, she began to dream of meeting someone. Someone special who would one day walk into her life. Someone she would instantly feel she had known for years. Someone who would feel the same about her.

THE STUFF THAT
NIGHTMARES ARE MADE OF

Masako was in the same class as Bunichi Morimoto again. They'd been in the same classes all the way through primary school, but had been placed in different ones the previous year, when they started secondary school. Bunichi had grown quite a lot in that past year, and now Masako only came up to his shoulders, so sometimes felt a little awkward standing next to him. But they were good friends who always spent their breaks working on their homework together. Their classmates teased them about this, but they didn't let it bother them.

One day, towards the end of summer, Masako was packing her books into her bag when Bunichi came up to her and asked, "Are you going to volleyball practice today?"

"No, I'm going home. I have way too much homework."

"We can go home together then, if you like," said Bunichi. "But won't your team-mates be upset that you skipped practice?"

"They won't mind. I'm too short to get much time on the court anyway, so I think it's okay to slack off a little from time to time."

And with that, the two of them walked out of the school gates side by side and onto the street, to where the sycamore leaves were already turning yellow and a cool breeze danced around them.

"Bunichi?" said Masako in the tone she reserved for asking favours. "Do you think you could help me with today's math homework?"

"Yeah, sure. Why don't you come over to my house?"

"No way!" cried out Masako, surprising even herself. It simply wasn't like her to react that way.

"There's no need to shout. I mean, you don't have to come if you don't want to."

"I'm sorry," said Masako, feeling bad. "I don't know what came over me."

"You're a strange one sometimes, Masako."

As they carried on walking, Masako wondered why she'd shouted like that. Was it that she really didn't want to go to Bunichi's house? There wasn't any reason for her to feel that way after all. So instead she searched her mind for an explanation and started to think of Bunichi's young and pretty mother, whom she hadn't seen in a while.

"I just... didn't want to disturb your mother," offered Masako.

"Oh, is that what you were worried about? That's *so* not like you!" said Bunichi, laughing. There wasn't much you could do to dampen Bunichi's spirits, and that was one of the things Masako liked about him.

"All right then," said Masako, "I guess I could stop by just for a little bit."

"Great!"

When they arrived, Bunichi's mother seemed a little surprised to see Masako.

"Why, Masako, it's been a while, hasn't it? I haven't seen you since your primary-school graduation ceremony!"

"Yes, it has been a while," said Masako, doing her best to sound older than she was.

"You're so tanned, and you haven't grown one bit!"

"Hey! I'm kind of self-conscious about my height, you know!" said Masako in a sulky tone.

Bunichi's mother laughed. "I'm sorry. It's just that Bunichi has grown so much this past year, so it's a little funny to see you haven't changed at all."

"Come on, let's go up to my room," said Bunichi impatiently.

As Masako followed Bunichi to his room, his mother called out from behind them. "And try not to faint this time, Masako!"

"Faint?" said Masako, turning around. "What do you mean?"

"Don't you remember? Last time you went into Bunichi's room, something startled you and you fainted."

That's right, thought Masako. She had seen something terrifying in Bunichi's room. But what was it that had scared her so much that she'd fainted?

"You know, I really don't remember what it was that startled me so badly."

"Maybe it was so scary that you erased it from your memory," said Bunichi's mother, laughing. "That's not so unusual, you know."

When Masako heard that, it made her not want to go into Bunichi's room.

"Bunichi?" she said. "That scary thing… is it still there?"

"Yeah, sure it is. Come up and see," he replied with a smirk on his face.

"No way!"

"Okay, then you wait here. I'll go ahead and put it away."

"Do you remember what it was?" Masako turned to Bunichi's mother, who was now pouring tea for them.

"Well," said Bunichi's mother, looking a little unsure. "I didn't really pay so much attention to what it was that scared you. My main concern was that you had fainted. I do recall that it was actually something quite silly, though."

"Masako!" called out Bunichi. "You can come in now."

"Are you sure you've put it away?" asked Masako as she anxiously approached the door.

"Yeah, it's fine. You can come in now."

Slowly and cautiously, Masako stepped into Bunichi's room. And as soon as she did, out jumped Bunichi from behind the door with a mask on his face! It was a "Prajna" mask from one of the stories Bunichi liked, with hollow eyes, a gaping bright-red mouth and an expression so fierce it could only belong to a creature from another world.

THE PRAJNA MASK

Masako let out a scream, pushed Bunichi out of her way and ran right past his mother and out of the front door – without even stopping to put on her shoes. She felt as if her heart might jump out of her mouth at any moment, and she didn't stop until she was a good ten metres away from the house, where she squatted down on the pavement and tried to catch her breath. Now she remembered all too well. That was the same stupid mask that had terrified her the last time! And how nasty was it of Bunichi to scare her like that! Perhaps he thought it was funny. Well, it most certainly was not! He should know how frightened she was of that mask!

"That's it," said Mariko to herself as her eyes became red, more from anger than fear. "I don't need his help with my homework any more. I'm never going to hang out with him ever again."

Mariko stood up and looked around. The street was completely empty, except for a single black cat that was sitting next to the mailbox. She wished she could just go home. But first she needed her shoes, so reluctantly she went back to Bunichi's house, and as she entered she heard Bunichi being scolded by his mother.

"What were you thinking!? Masako is a girl! That was way out of line, young man!"

"But..." Bunichi stammered. "I didn't think it would scare her so much. I mean, she's not a kid any more. If anything, I thought I would get a laugh out of her..."

Bunichi sounded genuinely confused and concerned.

"Stop making excuses and go look for her. Now!" his mother shouted.

"It's okay, I'm right here," said Masako, feeling a little sorry for him.

Both Bunichi and his mother hurried towards her, apologizing profusely as they came, and Masako started to feel a little embarrassed for making such a big deal over a small thing. As an apology, Bunichi offered to break his piggy bank and use the proceeds to take her to a movie on Sunday. Masako was happy and ready to accept his apology, but she thought she'd better stay in a sulk for just a little while longer. After all, if she went back to her usual mood too quickly, then Bunichi might tease her about the whole thing.

Several days had passed since the incident with the Prajna mask at Bunichi's house, but Masako couldn't stop thinking about it. The mask was certainly scary, no question about it. But it was just a mask after all. So Masako couldn't quite understand why she'd reacted in such an extreme manner. *What's so scary about a stupid mask?* she thought to herself. *Surely there must be a reason. Or could it be that I'm just more easily scared than others?*

As she mulled these thoughts over in her head, Masako remembered that Bunichi was afraid of something too. Spiders. Masako, on the other hand, had no problem with them. *I guess...* she pondered, *different people are just scared of different things.* But still, there was something about the incident with the mask that continued to bother her.

Thinking back to her first year of secondary school, Masako remembered a time when she'd had to draw a Prajna mask for art class. When she'd first seen the mask, she'd felt a shiver go down her spine, but she'd soon got used to it. So it seemed it was only scary to her now when it suddenly appeared in front of her. Perhaps it wouldn't be scary any more if she were to look at it for long enough. It also occurred to her, for the first time, that maybe the reason she didn't like art class was the fact that the walls of the art room were decorated with Prajna masks. She'd loved art class in primary school, after all. But in secondary school, she hadn't even bothered to join the art club. Instead, she'd decided to join the volleyball club, even though she wasn't any good at it. Perhaps there was something more to her feelings about the Prajna mask. Could it be that she'd had some terrible experience with a Prajna mask some time ago? An experience she could no longer remember?

THE WOMAN WITH SCISSORS

When it came to being easily scared, nobody was more easily scared than Masako's younger brother, Yoshio. He was almost five years old, but still he kept wetting his bed because he couldn't go to the toilet on his own at night – no matter how many times his parents told him off for it. Masako felt sorry for him, not only because he was always being told off by their parents, but also because his classmates had started to tease him and call him "bed-wetter". If only there was something she could do to help him stop wetting the bed! Several months earlier she had even asked Yoshio about it.

"Hey, Yoshio," she'd said. "Why is it you're so scared of going to the toilet?"

"Because it's so far from where I sleep," Yoshio had replied.

Yoshio did have a point. After all, they lived in a relatively large house, and the hallway leading to the bathroom was really quite long.

"And it's dark," Yoshio had added. "And there's something there too."

"What do you mean 'something'? Do you mean a ghost?"

"No, nothing like that."

"What then?"

"Something scary."

"Is it a person?"

"Yeah."

"A spirit of some kind?"

"No, not a spirit. It's a woman."

"Why would a woman scare you?"

"Because her hair is all messy and her face is pale and scary."

"It must be a spirit of some kind then."

"It's not."

"Well how do you know it's not a spirit?"

"I don't know *how* I know! I just know that it isn't."

"And this woman is in the hallway?"

"No, she's inside the bathroom. When I open the bathroom door, she's always standing there with a pair of scissors in her hand."

Yoshio looked genuinely terrified as he explained this to Masako.

"Why does she have a pair of scissors on her?"

"I don't know."

Now Masako was starting to feel a bit scared, too. She imagined this woman with crazy hair and a pale face, with the eyes of a fox and with a pair of scissors in her hand. Surely there was no way Yoshio could have imagined all that by himself. Somebody else must have told him to try and scare him.

"Who told you such a scary story?" Masako asked.

"Nobody," said Yoshio, shaking his head.

"So you made it up yourself?"

"I'm not making it up! She's really there!" Yoshio shouted, with tears welling up in his eyes.

Masako wondered if her mother or father might have told Yoshio such a story. First, she checked with her mother, but she knew nothing about it. Then, when Masako's father came home from work, she asked him too.

"Why would I tell him such a silly story?" said her father, visibly upset.

That night, Masako woke up in the middle of the night with an idea. She got out of bed and went over to Yoshio.

"Wake up, Yoshio!" she whispered. "It's time to go to

the bathroom. If you don't go now, you'll wet the bed again. Come on! I'll go with you!"

"No way," said Yoshio, his eyes peeping out from under the covers, "I'm scared."

"But there's no need to be," said Masako, reassuringly. "I'm telling you, there's nobody in there."

"Oh yes there will be," said Yoshio. "She'll be there."

If you don't go, you'll wet the bed again. Come on, we have to go."

The two of them got up and started walking down the long hallway towards the toilet. Masako was sure she could see Yoshio trembling.

"Yoshio, you really are a coward aren't you? Stop shaking!" said Masako, laughing. But, inside, Masako was a little scared as well. What if there really was someone in the bathroom? What if there was someone wearing a Prajna mask? If there was, she would surely scream!

As they carried on down the hallway with its squeaky floorboards underfoot, Yoshio held Masako's hand tight. His palm was now sweating and his body was trembling. When they finally reached the bathroom door, Yoshio squatted down on the floor and said, "I can't do it. I'm scared!"

"It's all right." Masako reassured him, but her voice was quivering slightly too. So without saying another word, she gripped Yoshio's hand tightly and slowly opened the bathroom door.

"You see?" said Masako. "There's no one here."

"That's because you're here," said Yoshio. "If I was alone, then she'd be here."

Masako wondered what she could do. How could she possibly convince her little brother that the woman in the bathroom didn't exist? She couldn't even convince herself that the stupid Prajna mask wasn't scary! Perhaps she needed to find out the reason behind both of their fears. Perhaps then they would be able to overcome them.

The following Sunday, on the way home from the movies, Masako decided to ask Bunichi for advice.

"Okay," said Bunichi, laughing, "so we've got a brother and sister and both of them are cowards."

Noticing that he was the only one laughing, Bunichi cleared his throat and spoke in a more serious voice.

"Actually," he continued, "my uncle is a psychologist, and he once told me that when people find out the cause of their fear, then that fear usually goes away. So maybe that's the key to Yoshio stopping his bed-wetting."

Encouraged by Bunichi's words, Masako decided
to get to work on doing something about her little brother's fears as well as her own. Maybe then
the other boys her brother's age would stop teasing
him and let him join in with their games. Then he
wouldn't always have to play indoor games with the
girls nearby, such as Atsuko, who lived across the
street, or Hisako, who lived two houses down the
road. Masako's mother would be happy too. She was
quite a tough woman, and was a little embarrassed
about her little crybaby son.

Later that day, Masako and her mother were sitting
in the living room – with Masako reading a book and
her mother busy with her craftwork – when all of a
sudden Yoshio came running in with tears trickling
down his cheeks.

"Oh Yoshio!" said their mother. "Have you been bul-
lied again?"

"I was playing with Hisako and Atsuko, and Hiro
called me a sissy!" said Yoshio between sobs.

Hiro was a first-grader and the biggest bully in their
neighbourhood. But their mother was sick of hearing
this kind of thing and was in no mood to cheer her
son up.

"Oh come on now, Yoshio! I hope you didn't just come running home without saying anything back to him!"

Yoshio stopped rubbing his eyes and dropped his hands to his sides.

"I *did* say something! I said I'm *not* a sissy!"

"And?"

"And then he kicked my book." And with that, little Yoshio started to sob again.

"That's awful!" said Masako, standing up. "I'm going to go have a word with Hiro!"

"No, Masako," said their mother. "You stay here."

A SCOLDING FROM MUM

"You're a boy, Yoshio!" said his mother. "You need to start acting like one. You can't keep crying and running home like this. You know they pick on you because you're always playing with girls. Why don't you join in with the boys and play their games?"

Masako watched as her mother started to rant. Once she started, there was no telling how long she would go on for, and Yoshio had already started to sob again.

"Boys need to have the courage to fight back!" their mother continued. "If you want to keep on playing with girls all the time, I'm going to have to snip off your weenie!"

"Oh!" gasped Masako.

"What's the matter?" said her mother, slightly annoyed at having her lecture interrupted.

"I know why Yoshio is afraid of going to the bathroom, and why he always wets his bed! It's because of what you say when you tell him off for playing with the girls!"

"What?" said their mother, looking first to Masako, then to Yoshio.

"The scary woman Yoshio sees in the bathroom at night – it's you, Mum! And the reason she's always holding scissors is because, well you know, the scissors are for…"

Masako watched her mother's face change as she slowly put the pieces together.

"Oh, so what you're saying is that the scissors are for cutting off Yoshio's weenie?"

Yoshio, who had since stopped sobbing, looked up at his mother, while Masako and her mother looked back at him. For a moment there was silence, then both Masako and her mother burst out laughing at Yoshio's quizzical expression.

"You know what that means, don't you Yoshio?" said Masako, pulling herself together. "It means you just made that woman up in your mind because of what Mum said to you. Do you see? That means there's not really a woman there at all, so there's no need for you to be scared any more!"

"Oh, I see," said Yoshio, though it wasn't clear if he really understood or not.

Yoshio's mother didn't say anything, but she seemed to be feeling bad about the careless choice of words that had scared her son so much. And though Yoshio didn't entirely understand what had just happened, he did at least understand that there was no woman in the bathroom to be afraid of. So from that day on, he was always able to go to the toilet all by himself, even in the middle of the night, and he never wet his bed again. As for Masako, she was surprised at how well she'd been able to help Yoshio overcome his fear. Now she felt even more determined to conquer her own.

A FEAR OF HEIGHTS

When Masako sat down and thought about it, the Prajna mask wasn't the only thing she was afraid of. She was also pretty scared of heights. To be fair, quite a lot of people are scared of heights. But in Masako's case, the fear was a bit more extreme. Even if she had a really firm grip on the handrail, she could never bring herself to look down whenever she was standing somewhere high up. She'd certainly tried on many occasions to have a look at the ground far below. But somehow she was scared that if she did, then she might suddenly feel a strange and sudden urge to climb over the rail and step off. And just the thought of that made her want to scream. There were also many cases where she was too afraid to even grab hold of the handrail. After all, what if the part she was holding on to suddenly were to break off and send her plummeting face down to the ground below?

I can't always act like a child, she thought to herself. *I have to overcome this silly fear as soon as possible. What I need to do is to find somewhere really high up, somewhere that doesn't even have handrails. Then I need to force myself to climb up! But what if I suddenly get dizzy up there? I might fall! Maybe I should ask Bunichi to come with me. Just to be safe.*

A couple of days later, on the way home from school, Masako told Bunichi about her idea.

"You're scared of a lot of things, aren't you Masako?" he replied, unhelpfully.

"So what if I am? I can't help it, can I?" she said. "But at least I can try to do something about it. Or would you prefer I try to do something about *your* fear, huh? I could drop a few spiders down the back of your shirt and see how you like that!"

Bunichi turned pale at the bare mention of the word "spider".

"No no, please, anything but that," he pleaded. "I can't stand spiders. Just thinking about them makes me sick!"

"See! Even you are afraid of things. So how about it? Will you climb somewhere really high with me?"

"Yeah, I'll go. So long as you promise me you won't ever do what you just said. You know, with the... spiders."

"Okay, I'll let you off."

"But where do you have in mind? Do you even know of anywhere high that doesn't have any handrails?"

Masako actually did know just the place.

"The clock tower, of course!"

"What?! That's so dangerous," said Bunichi, clearly taken aback. The clock tower was located on the roof of their school. It was an old tower, with the hands on the clock permanently stuck at 9:15, and it was about three storeys high!

"But that place is off limits!" Bunichi said with a worried look on his face. "Because it's so dangerous!"

When Masako and Bunichi reached the stairs that led to the machine room at the back of the clock tower, they noticed how very narrow they were. And not only were they narrow, but there were no handrails along the stairs and no walls on either side! Perhaps it had been designed that way to make it easy to build, but it certainly wasn't designed for being very safe.

"Are you going to go up there?" asked Bunichi.

"Of course. Why, are you scared?"

"Of course I'm not scared! I just don't want us to be caught and get into trouble, that's all."

"Don't worry. The place is only off-limits because they're worried about boys like you going up there and being stupid and reckless," said Masako, determined to convince Bunichi. "But we're just going to go up there and then come right back down."

"But off-limits is off-limits!"

"And rules are there to be broken," said Masako, bringing the conversation to an end. It didn't matter to her that her argument made no sense at all.

THE CLOCK TOWER

When they reached the roof, the autumn breeze blew a chill through their clothes, and they stood for a moment together, gazing up at the tower.

"Can you climb up that high?" asked Bunichi.

"No problem," said Masako with false confidence, as she did her best to stop her legs from shaking. Then off she went inside the tower with an air of cheerfulness that was just as false.

"Hey, hold on," called out Bunichi behind her. "It's dangerous, let's go together."

As they climbed the dusty steps, Masako took in the view. She could see the low green hills on the outskirts of town, all the different shades of foliage under the autumn sky and the long white strip of road that snaked its way into town – past the church, the fire station and the watchtower – and then wound its way to the front door of the school.

"Oh!" Masako let out a gasp as she suddenly felt dizzy and needed to rest on the stairs.

"You shouldn't look down," said Bunichi, grabbing her shoulders. "What should we do, Masako?" he asked her. "Should we go back down?"

But they had already got quite far up. In fact, there was only one floor left until they reached the machine room. Masako decided it would be a shame to turn back, so she shook her head and said, "No, let's keep going!"

"But you can't even stand up!"

"Well then, please can you take my hand?"

Bunichi hesitantly reached out to take her hand and helped her to her feet, then slowly they continued their ascent. As they went, there were several landings between flights of stairs, each with an overhang and a concrete divider about forty centimetres high, and when they reached the last one, there were only twenty steps left to the machine room. But right at that moment, Bunichi – who had been walking ahead of Masako – let out a piercing scream, let go of Masako's hand and started waving his arms around frantically.

"It's a spi... A spi... spider's web!" he blurted out pointing to a huge cobweb in the corner of the landing.

"Be careful!" yelled Masako.

But Bunichi was too busy grappling with the spider's web to even notice how close his feet were getting to the concrete divider. He lost his footing, tripped over the divider, and his body went sailing over the overhang.

"Help," cried Bunichi.

"Oh no!" screamed Masako, forgetting her fear and scrambling to the edge, where Bunichi's fingers were clinging on. "Hang on tight, Bunichi!"

Bravely, Masako grabbed hold of both of Bunichi's hands and tried to pull him up with all her strength. She knew that, if he were to lose his grip, then both of them would end up falling several flights to the ground.

If he falls, thought Masako, *it will be just awful. I brought him here, so it would be all my fault. And I'll die as well!*

Fortunately, Bunichi managed to swing one of his legs onto the overhang, so Masako was able to grab him by the belt and pull him in.

For several moments they sat on the narrow overhang in silence, looking at each other, listening to their hearts pounding away and waiting for their breathing to return to normal. Both of them were thinking about what might have happened, and both of them felt a chill run down their spine.

It's weird, thought Masako, *but I feel that something like this happened once before.*

THE SCARY BRIDGE

"You know what?" Masako said to Bunichi several days later. "I'm not at all scared of heights any more."

"Well, my psychologist uncle told me that people can sometimes have fears that come from guilt. So maybe your sense of guilt was replaced by the wonderful fact that you saved my life!"

"A sense of guilt, huh?" Masako wondered out loud.

Masako thought about what Bunichi had said. Could she have done something bad when she was much younger? Something she was too young to remember? Or could it be that she hadn't done anything wrong, but something bad had happened and left her with a sense of guilt that had remained until that day? Perhaps it was some sort of secret from long ago. Something related to a Prajna mask and high places perhaps? But where could such a place be? And what could have happened? No matter how hard Masako tried to remember, nothing came to mind. Even though she had felt that something similar had happened before when Bunichi almost fell from the clock tower.

Several weeks later, just after the end of the autumn festival, Masako and Bunichi took a walk along the river that ran by the side of the town. The red spider lilies that had bloomed so beautifully in summer were nothing more than a memory now, and the two of them made their way down to the edge of the river to skim stones, before making their way over to the foot of a long bridge.

"Masako?" said Bunichi. "You know, it's still early. Shall we walk across the bridge and down into the suburbs?"

"Yeah, sure," said Masako. But then she noticed that the rails on both sides of the bridge were very low. "Actually, I think it might be time to head back," she added, feeling that indescribable fear coming back.

"Why?"

"Just because."

"Do you have other plans?"

"No, not particularly."

"Then why not?" said Bunichi, suddenly noticing the anxious look on her face. "You're not going to start telling me that you're scared of crossing the bridge, are you?"

Bunichi had hit the nail on the head – so Masako didn't even bother to reply. Instead, she glanced at the long white bridge, with its telegraph poles dotted along it at intervals of several metres and the low, wooden rails in between. Masako was now getting quite scared. *Something like this has happened before!* She thought to herself. *And something bad is now about to happen.*

"I don't want to cross the bridge," Masako suddenly said.

"You really are a strange one," said Bunichi as he took a few steps onto the bridge and peered over the handrail into the waters below.

"I guess it is a little high up," he added. "But then, I thought you'd already overcome your fear of heights."

"I just don't like this bridge!"

"Suit yourself."

Bunichi peered over the edge again and listened carefully. There was nobody around except for the two of them, and all he could hear was the rushing of the water and the occasional croak from a frog.

"I've got it!" said Bunichi. "It's not heights you're afraid of it. It's the rails and handrails in high places that scare you! You were able to climb up that clock tower because there were no rails! Don't you see – that made it easier for you!"

"But why would I be scared of rails?"

"I don't know. But there are plenty of people who have random phobias."

Masako wasn't sure if Bunichi was making fun of her, so she started to pout a little.

"Well, I can't help what I find scary, can I! I just feel as if something might come jumping out from behind one of those telegraph poles."

"What, like someone wearing a Prajna mask?" smirked Bunichi.

"Stop it!" yelled Masako, surprising Bunichi.

"What's wrong?"

"Look, I'm scared! I'm really scared!"

Masako covered her face with both hands and sank down onto the ground. She suddenly felt like she might be able to remember something that happened a long time ago. But at the same time, she was too scared to remember it.

"Are you not feeling well?" asked Bunichi, looking genuinely worried.

Masako said nothing, but gave a small nod.

"Okay then," said Bunichi. "Let's go home."

THE HEAD IN THE HALLWAY

Masako felt as if she could remember whatever it was that had happened if she really put her mind to it. But she was afraid the memory might be too painful for her to bear. So several frustrating days went by. It was actually during that period that Yoshio started to wet his bed again.

"What is it this time?" asked Masako. "The woman with the scissors isn't there any more, right?"

"No, she isn't..." replied Yoshio. "It's just that..." Yoshio's voice trailed off into incomprehensible mumbling.

Later on, long after they'd gone to bed, Masako awoke in the middle of the night and tried again to help Yoshio overcome his fear.

"Come on, Yoshio," she said, shaking him awake, "let's take you to the bathroom."

"But..." Yoshio mumbled, sleepily.

"Come on, hurry up, or you're going to wet the bed again."

"But I don't want to go yet."

"But you have to go. Oh… I see. You're scared again, aren't you? You're back to being a big scaredy-cat!"

"No, that's not why."

"Well then, go!"

Yoshio pulled back the covers and got out of bed. Then he walked out into the hallway slowly. As for Masako, she was feeling quite satisfied with herself, so she rolled over onto her side and closed her eyes. But before she could fall back to sleep, Yoshio came back into the room with his face as pale as a sheet. Then he sat down next to Masako and began to cry.

"What's the matter?" asked Masako, surprised.

"At the corner of the hallway, there's a man's head on the floor," sobbed Yoshio.

"What?" said Masako, sitting upright. "That's impossible. You must have just dreamt it!"

"No, it's really there… covered in blood, and rolling around on the floor."

Overwhelmed with fear, Yoshio threw himself into Masako's arms, trembling. Masako tried to be brave, but she was so scared by Yoshio's story that she had to make an effort to stop her teeth from chattering.

FATHER'S SECRET

"But it really can't be true," said Masako, trying to convince herself as well as Yoshio. "A man's head in the hallway. I mean, it just can't be true."

But Yoshio seemed genuinely terrified. He wasn't playing.

For a moment, Masako considered going to the bathroom with Yoshio again. But what would she do if there really was a man's head on the floor? She even considered waking her parents, who were asleep in the next room, and asking them to come along as well. But if she did that, then Yoshio would know she was scared as well, and she didn't want that. She needed to be strong for his sake, so she could set a good example – no matter how scared she really was inside.

"I'll show you how ridiculous it is," she said, hopping out of bed.

"You're not really going, are you?" said Yoshio with

his eyes wide-open. "You're not really going to go to the bathroom?"

"Yes I am."

With that, Masako took hold of Yoshio's wrists and tried to make him stand. But Yoshio wouldn't move. In fact, he was so scared that his body was frozen still, so he couldn't get out of bed even if he'd wanted to.

What a wimp, thought Masako, *I can't believe he's a boy!*

After reassuring Yoshio that everything would be fine, Masako stepped out into the hallway with Yoshio in tow. There was no light out there, and in the dark, for just a second, she felt as if there might actually be something there. But she'd never been scared to go to the bathroom before, so she was determined not to be frightened this time either.

"Things look scary only because you think they're scary," she whispered to Yoshio.

Together, they peered around the corner of the hallway and along to the bathroom.

"See!" said Masako. "There's nothing there."

Yoshio blinked his eyes and grabbed hold of his sister's body, then took a good long look along the hallway.

"That's so strange," he said. "I swear it was there earlier."

Masako wondered why on earth Yoshio might have imagined a man's head lying in the hallway. Surely there had to be a reason. But she knew there'd be no point in asking Yoshio, who most likely didn't know the answer himself.

It's amazing how the human mind works, Masako thought to herself, *it's just baffling!*

When the next morning came, Masako left the house together with her father, just like she did every day. The train station was on her way to school, so she could walk and chat with him every morning. Masako really enjoyed those chats, and she felt particularly close to her father. So she figured it would be all right to tell him about what had happened the night before. She thought he might even know how to help Yoshio overcome his fears. But unfortunately, her father knew more about engineering than he did about heads on hallway floors, so he was unable to suggest anything.

When they reached the station, Masako said goodbye to her father and carried on walking over the level crossing. For no particular reason, she turned to look back at the station, and when she did she got a bit of a surprise – she could see her father standing on the platform just like every other morning, but this time he was on the wrong platform waiting for a train going in the opposite direction. Masako wondered if he'd been deep in thought and gone there accidentally, but that seemed unlikely.

What's going on? thought Masako. *Maybe he just needs to stop by somewhere before work. But then, if that was the case, surely he would have left the house earlier than normal.*

Masako couldn't help but wonder whether she'd just seen something she wasn't supposed to, so she quickly turned around before her father could see her looking. And when she got to school, the thought still bothered her. All day long she kept wondering why her father wasn't going to work and why he was hiding something. In fact, she wondered so much, it was almost impossible to concentrate on her classes.

"Hey Masako!" said Bunichi a little later on. "Are you all right? You don't look well."

"Oh, I'm fine," said Masako, but Bunichi wasn't convinced.

VOICES IN THE NIGHT

All day long, Masako had wondered whether she should tell her mother about the incident at the station. And by the time she arrived home, she'd decided it was the right thing to do. Funnily enough, though, her mother didn't seem in the least bit surprised.

"Well Masako, there's something I didn't tell you about before, because I didn't want you to worry," she said with a frown on her face.

"What is it?"

"Well, it's not such a big deal as it might sound, but your father quit his job."

"He did? Why?"

"Well, his company didn't have as much work to do as they had before, so they needed to let some of the workers go."

"Let them go? But that means he didn't quit, right? He was fired!"

"I guess so. But there's really nothing to worry about.

Your father is lucky. He's a skilled engineer. So he'll have no trouble at all finding a new job. In fact, he's already received an offer from another company."

"Oh, I see."

Masako couldn't help but think it might have been better for her parents to tell her what was going on.

I'm an adult, too, she thought to herself, *so I'm old enough to be told things as important as that.* She felt especially frustrated with her father, and wished he would stop seeing her as just a child. So she decided to confront him about this on the way to the station the next day.

"So, dad, have you already decided on your next job?" she said, out of the blue.

Her father's eyes widened in surprise.

"Oh, so you know about that?" he said, then laughed out loud. "I guess you must have overheard me when I came home the other night, did you? I came home a little drunk and was probably talking louder than I should have, and complaining about how the company was going to 'give me the chop'. I probably woke you up."

Suddenly, Masako understood where Yoshio's night vision might have come from.

"Did you say 'give me the chop'?" she asked in a voice that was also a little too loud.

"I did," answered her father. "But there's no need to shout!"

"But I figured it out! The head Yoshio saw – it was yours!"

Poor little Yoshio must have overheard his father's voice in his sleep and conjured up the image of a bloody severed head. Masako couldn't help but giggle at how silly the whole episode had been, and so she told her father all about it.

"But this time might be a bit more difficult than last time," she continued. "We need to tell Yoshio that you were fired. Then we need to tell him that there's nothing to worry about."

Masako's father smiled and patted her on the shoulders with his large, warm hands.

"Oh Masako," he said with a proud look on his face. "You're such a clever girl. A born psychologist!"

THE NIGHTMARE TAKES SHAPE

Masako found herself standing alone on the bridge. The low wooden rails were old, and some were rotting or even broken. She could see the telegraph poles on one side at regular ten-metre intervals, and she slowly made her way down the middle of the bridge with the hairs on her neck standing on end. She was so very afraid. But she needed to cross the bridge to do the shopping for her mother. If only she could walk across with her eyes closed. But if she did, she might walk into one of those rotting rails and plunge down into the icy waters below. So instead she kept her eyes wide-open and fixed her gaze on the snow-capped mountains in the distance.

Why is everything so scary? she thought to herself. *What is it that's frightening me?*

But no matter how hard she thought about it, Masako couldn't figure it out. Then, suddenly, she froze on the spot. There was something hiding behind one of those telegraph poles! Something that just moved!

"Who is it? Who's there?" asked Masako, her voice trembling.

Then, at that very moment, something in a white cloth leapt out from behind the telegraph pole and gave a terrifying cry before landing right in front of Masako, where it studied her carefully through its fierce-looking Prajna mask.

For a moment, Masako stood rooted to the spot, too scared to even scream. Then she decided to run for her life. But her legs wouldn't move the way she wanted them to. Her knees were trembling, and each step was unsteady. Then one of her feet got caught in something, and she tumbled head first onto the railing – smashing right through it and over the edge into darkness. The sound of gushing water came closer and closer, and somewhere a voice called out.

"Etsuko!"

Who on earth is Etsuko, she thought to herself as she fell. *Is it someone I should know?*

Then the icy waters engulfed her and dragged her body deeper and deeper.

Masako woke up with a start. Her chest was pounding and she was gasping for air.

A dream! she thought. *It was only a dream!*

But what an awful nightmare it had been. Her pyjamas were soaked with sweat, but fortunately Yoshio was still fast asleep beside her. Quietly, she got out of bed, changed into a new pair of pyjamas and crawled back under the covers. But, as much as she tried, she couldn't get back to sleep.

Ha! Now I remember, she thought to herself. *Etsuko was a friend back from when we lived in the countryside. She was a cute girl. I must have been six and Etsuko five when we last saw each other. I wonder what she's doing now?*

The next morning, Masako woke up earlier than usual. She decided to take the longer route to school and invited Bunichi to walk with her. As they walked side by side, Masako recounted her nightmare from the previous night. She thought Bunichi might be able to tell her something about her dream, since he seemed to have learnt so much about such things from his psychologist uncle.

"I think something must have happened back when you lived in the countryside," said Bunichi after giving it some thought.

"I think so too," nodded Masako.

"And what about that girl, Etsuko? Do you think she still lives there?"

"Yeah, I think so."

"Is this place far?"

"No, you can get there and back in a day."

"Masako, you should go there this weekend," said Bunichi, stopping in his tracks. "I really think you'll find some answers if you do. You'll find out whatever it is that's troubling you so much."

Masako looked Bunichi straight in the eyes and said, "Will you come with me?"

"Of course I will."

"Thanks," said Masako, dropping her gaze. She was so happy to be returning to the place she'd loved after so many years away. And to go there with Bunichi was even better. But at the same time, she was a little worried about whatever horrible secrets she might find there.

Over the next few days, Masako wrestled with her mixed feelings. Then, when Sunday came, the weather was perfect, with not a single cloud in the sky. Bunichi came to pick her up early in the morning, and he seemed pleasantly surprised to see her wearing a very colourful dress.

"Wow!" said Bunichi. "You actually look like a proper girl with that on!"

"How rude!" pouted Masako. "What do you normally think of me as?"

"A girl, of course."

"Well," replied Masako, "you've also dressed up more than usual, haven't you."

Bunichi looked down at his new dark-green sweater as his cheeks turned bright-red in embarrassment.

Together they walked along until they reached the train station, where they took the local line downtown. Then they changed to another train, from where they watched the city fade away through the windows to be replaced by beautiful countryside scenes, with the leaves of trees changing to a palette of different colours and the rice fields glowing the brilliant gold of the harvest season.

"Do your grandparents still live in the countryside?" asked Bunichi, turning to Masako.

"No, we don't have family there any more. Apparently some people we don't know are living in the house we used to live in. But there are a lot of people we knew in the neighbourhood, so I'm sure they will all remember me."

"So you were born there?"

"Yeah, I lived there until I was six. After that my dad got his job, and we moved out into town."

A full four hours later, they arrived at their destination, where they took a quick lunch at a small restaurant along the shopping avenue near the station, then slowly started on their one-kilometre walk to the village where Masako was born. Behind them, the sun shone across the low mountains and hills nearby, and the air was clear and refreshing. On either side of the road there were fields of radishes and turnips, but there was not a soul in sight – perhaps because it was lunchtime.

"After we cross that river," said Masako, "there's not much further to go."

Masako felt conflicting emotions rising within her. She was excited to be back, but felt uneasy about what might lie ahead.

As they climbed the slope of the riverbank, Masako was surprised to see how wide and deep the river was. There was a long bridge that ran across it, and she remembered the bridge being there. But she hadn't seen it in such a long time, and now that she was looking at it again, she noticed its low wooden rails on both sides, which were rotten and broken in various places. She looked at the telegraph poles dotted along the bridge at ten-metre intervals, and past the bridge she could make out the shape of the snow-capped mountain range beyond.

This is it! she thought. *This is the bridge that appeared in my nightmare!*

Masako's feelings of nostalgia turned to fear, and her legs refused to carry her any farther forward.

Bunichi stopped as well and looked at Masako with cool, thoughtful eyes.

"It's this bridge, isn't it?" he said. "The one you saw in your dream."

"Yes," was all Masako managed to say.

"Come on, let's go!" said Bunichi. "Let's cross the bridge."

Masako wished she could say no. But if she were to turn back now, then she'd miss out on the chance to shed light on the darkness inside her. Then she thought back on how she'd urged her little brother to face his fears and walk along the hallway, and she started to feel a little embarrassed.

"Okay, I'll go," she said, reaching out reluctantly to Bunichi, who grabbed her hand firmly and began walking just a little ahead of her.

"Be careful not to touch the rails!" said Masako with a tremble in her voice.

"Don't worry," said Bunichi, "we'll just walk down the middle of the bridge."

Together they carried on for several more careful steps, with Bunichi leading the way and Masako keeping her eyes fixed firmly on her feet. Then Bunichi turned around and stopped.

"Masako, that's not going to work," he said with a frown. "You have to look around more and try to remember as much as you can."

"But I can't!" said Masako, covering her face with her hands. "I have this bad feeling that what happened in my dream will happen here! The poles will come tumbling down! Oh and there's someone standing behind that pole! See, something is going to jump out!"

It was then that they heard a voice nearby – a girl's voice.

"Masako! You're Masako, aren't you?"

A FACE FROM CHILDHOOD

Masako dropped her hands from her face in surprise
and looked towards the girl who was calling her name.
The voice belonged to a girl much taller than Masako.
She wore pigtails and a school uniform, and she was
standing about five metres away, staring right at them.

"Etsuko! You're Etsuko, aren't you?" Masako blurted
out, her feelings of nostalgia resurfacing.

Etsuko had grown into a pretty girl with smooth skin.
She was much taller now, but she still had the same big
eyes and full cheeks she'd had as a young child. Masako
was sure she'd recognize her anywhere and that Etsuko
would recognize Masako anywhere too. Masako wanted
to run up and give her a hug. But instead, she hesitated.
It had been such a very long time since they'd last seen
each other, and Masako felt a little shy. But it was okay,
because Etsuko seemed to be feeling the same way as well.
So, slowly, the two of them walked towards each other.

"You've grown so much," said Masako.

"I know. I'm like a telegraph pole, aren't I!"

Together they laughed and, inside, Masako felt quite relieved. *She hasn't changed one bit!* she thought to herself.

Masako and Etsuko grabbed each other's hands in delight, and Bunichi gave a small but purposeful cough, prompting Masako to introduce him.

"This is my classmate. Bunichi Morimoto. And this is Etsuko Kitajima. You remember I told you about her?"

Bunichi took an awkward step forward and stiffly introduced himself.

"I've heard a lot about you from Masako," said Bunichi in his best adult-like voice, forcing Masako to stifle a giggle.

Etsuko blushed a little and bowed her head.

"How many years has it been?" asked Masako.

"Let me see..." said Etsuko, walking over to the wooden railing. "It must be seven... no, eight years now! I often thought about you. We were such good friends, but you never came back to see us."

"I'm sorry. I often thought of you as well. You were even in my dream."

Masako tried to take a step towards Etsuko, but stopped in her tracks. The railing behind Etsuko was rotten and weak, and she was afraid it might break off.

"But now we've finally been reunited!" said Etsuko, walking over to Masako and taking her hands in hers. "I was so worried that you were still upset about that incident."

Masako was startled to hear Etsuko's words, and she quickly glanced back to Bunichi.

"What do you mean, 'that incident'?" asked Bunichi as he stepped towards Etsuko with a serious look on his face.

Masako's pulse was racing. What was this mysterious incident? Was it the cause of Masako's troubled emotions? Did Etsuko hold the key to unlock Masako's nightmares?

"What's the matter?" said Bunichi. "You both look so serious... You're scaring me."

Without thinking, Masako placed both hands firmly on Etsuko's shoulders. Etsuko grimaced in pain.

"Please, tell me! What happened? What do you mean by 'the incident'?"

"You're hurting me!" cried Etsuko. "Let me go!"

But Masako was far too caught up in her need for answers. In fact, she was shaking Etsuko by the shoulders without even realizing it. Fortunately, Bunichi stepped in and took Masako's hands in his.

"Ow, that hurt," said Etsuko, rubbing her shoulders and throwing a glare in Masako's direction. "You didn't come here to see me, did you? What did you come here for? Don't tell me you don't remember what happened."

"Look," said Bunichi. "I don't know what happened between you two. But Masako is struggling because she can't remember what the incident was."

"Are you serious?" asked Etsuko, looking beyond Bunichi's shoulders to where Masako was standing, about to burst into tears. "You really have forgotten?"

Masako nodded sadly.

"I'm disappointed," said Etsuko with a downcast look on her face, then she turned her back to them and walked over to the rail again.

All three of them stood for a while in silence, listening to the sounds of frogs and wondering what to do next. Then, finally, unable to stand the silence any longer, Bunichi decided to speak out.

"Listen, Etsuko," he said. "Masako is feeling bad about something. But she doesn't know what it is or why. Please can you try to understand?"

"And I'm sorry for becoming hysterical like that too," added Masako.

"Etsuko?" continued Bunichi. "Whatever it was that happened between you two, did it happen here on this bridge?"

"Did somebody fall perhaps?" asked Masako, timidly.

Etsuko whipped her head around and shot Masako a nasty glare.

"Did somebody fall, you ask?" she shouted, pointing at Masako. "You threw me off the bridge!"

A BRIDGE ACROSS MEMORIES

Masako couldn't believe her ears. She shook her head again and again, wishing it would all go away and, without realizing, she took a step backward, then another, then another.

"No way! That can't be true!" she said to herself. "There's no way I would ever do such a thing."

"Masako," said Bunichi in a worried voice.

Then, suddenly, Masako let out a long and lingering scream – splitting the silence around them. In a flash, she remembered. She remembered everything, and the shock of it all sent her running.

"Hey, where are you going?" called out Bunichi behind her. "Watch out!"

Masako was running and stumbling, with her hands wiping the tears that ran from her eyes. But fortunately, by the time she had reached the end of the bridge, Bunichi caught up with her.

"What do you think you're doing?" he said. "That's so

dangerous. You weren't looking where you were going! What if you'd run into one of those rails?"

"I didn't mean to!" cried Masako as Bunichi put his arms around her. "I didn't do it on purpose."

It had all happened eight years ago, when Masako was only seven years old. It was autumn, but it had been a humid day, with the distant mountain range turning grey under cloudy skies and rain threatening to fall at any moment. No one else was there, and there wasn't a sound, except for the cries of the frogs by the water below. Masako was on her way home, having finished the shopping her mother had asked her to do at the other end of the bridge, and she was walking deliberately down the middle – as her mother had always told her to – away from the dangerous rails along the sides. That was when it happened.

"Do you remember?" asked Bunichi, kindly, and Masako gave a sheepish nod.

Etsuko, who had been running behind Bunichi, caught up.

"Masako! I'm sorry! I had no idea you were suffering so much! I mean, it happened eight years ago!"

"But I remember! Etsuko, I remember now!"

"But it was my fault!" said Etsuko, gripping Masako's hand. "That day, I'd taken the Prajna mask hanging on my father's wall without asking. I thought I could wear it and surprise someone. That's why I was hiding behind the pole on that bridge. But it wasn't like I was planning to play a prank on you. I was just waiting for the first person to cross the bridge. It could've been anyone. I didn't even know it was you until I came out from behind the pole. Please believe me!"

Masako played the incident again in her mind: Etsuko jumping out in front of her with the Prajna mask on and her hair flailing wildly in the autumn breeze. She remembered how she'd screamed in sheer terror, and how she'd pushed Etsuko in the chest with all her strength. She recalled the sound of Etsuko's back hitting the rail behind her and the crack of the wood giving way behind her. How Etsuko had seemed to hang in mid-air for just a moment before plunging with a scream into the waters below.

EVENTS THAT FOLLOWED

"Luckily, I fainted while I was falling," said Etsuko, "so I didn't actually swallow much water."

Masako tried hard to listen, but Etsuko's voice seemed as if it were coming from far away.

"Then I floated a little way downriver and came to rest on the bank," continued Etsuko, putting her hand gently on Masako's shoulder, "and that's where somebody found me. Luckily, it was someone I knew, so they carried me straight back home. Unfortunately, I ended up getting pneumonia, so I was bedridden for quite a long time. But by the time I'd finally recovered, you were already gone. Your family had already moved into town."

"I felt so alone," sniffed Masako, with her eyes still staring blankly into the distance. "After I pushed you into the river, I ran back home crying. And after that I came down with a fever. All the time I was in bed I kept having horrible dreams. I was delirious and talking in my sleep. And when I was finally able to get up…"

Masako's voice trailed off and she hung her head.

"And then you didn't remember what happened, right?" said Bunichi, stepping in to help his friend explain. "You'd forgotten everything!"

"That's right," Masako nodded.

"When you threw Etsuko off the bridge, you thought you killed her," Bunichi continued. "The feeling of guilt was so strong that you couldn't handle it, so unconsciously you erased everything from your memory."

Bunichi was exactly right. Masako must have been so worried about Etsuko that she'd come down with a fever and felt so bad about what had happened that she'd erased it from her memory. But somehow, she'd always remained afraid of Prajna masks. Or was she? Perhaps it wasn't that she was afraid of Prajna masks at all. Perhaps she was simply afraid that the mask might make her remember the terrible incident. Maybe that was why she was scared of heights too. And maybe that was why saving Bunichi from falling hadn't been enough to cure that fear of heights – but it had served to remind her that something like that had happened before and that there was somebody else who needed saving.

Now everything was clear to Masako – everything that had happened that day. It was as if the mists had risen from her mind and set her emotions free to settle down again. Masako took a breath, then she looked up and smiled at Bunichi and Etsuko.

"I'm all right now. Again, I'm so sorry for making you worry."

Bunichi and Etsuko both looked relieved.

"Etsuko, I did a horrible thing to you, didn't I?" said Masako, taking Etsuko's hand and blushing with embarrassment.

"No, it's okay."

"Thanks, Bunichi-san," continued Masako with unusual politeness. "It's all thanks to you."

"You're so silly, Masako," said Bunichi, turning bright red again.

"Hey, why don't you guys come over to my house?" said Etsuko suddenly, brightening the mood. "We have lots of fruit!"

Masako remembered how every autumn Etsuko's house was filled with pears and grapes sent from friends of her family who worked in an orchard, and together the three of them headed towards her house – walking in a single line down the middle of the bridge, with Etsuko's pigtails swaying in the cool mountain breeze.

YOSHIO STANDS UP

About a week after her visit to the countryside, Masako was walking home from school when she came across Hisako, Atsuko and Yoshio squatting down on the ground and playing a game together.

"Here we go," said Masako to herself, "playing with the girls again."

But Masako didn't really mind. In fact, seeing them all playing together and having fun made her feel warm and happy inside.

I wonder what it is they're playing? she thought to herself. And with that, she decided to hide behind a nearby wall and listen in on them.

"You must be tired after a long day," said Atsuko in a surprisingly grown-up voice.

"Yes, I'm exhausted," replied Yoshio, imitating his father's usual comment on returning home every night, and nearly making Masako laugh out loud.

"Did you do your homework?" asked Atsuko.

"Yes, I did," replied Hisako.

So Yoshio is playing the father, thought Masako. *Atsuko is playing the mother and Hisako is playing the child.*

Suddenly, Yoshio called out in a loud voice.

"I was fired from my job today. But I don't mind one bit. Another company insists that I join them. So I don't care that they asked me to leave."

Yoshio made it sound as if it was fun to be fired, and Masako buried her face in her bag to stifle her giggles. When she finally felt as if she could breathe without giggling, she lifted her face from her bag and listened in carefully again. But it had suddenly fallen very quiet. So Masako decided to sneak a peek over the wall to see what was going on.

When she lifted her eyes above the top of the wall, Masako saw that the three children had fallen silent. They weren't playing their game any more, and she could see another boy walking towards them. *Oh no!* thought Masako. *It's Hiro! The number-one bully in the neighbourhood!*

"So the sissy is playing with the girls again, eh?" said Hiro in a mocking voice. "What a wimp!"

Hisako opened her picture book and started to read it, hoping Hiro might go away. But Atsuko and Yoshio kept their eyes fixed on him as he came closer.

"If you keep playing with girls, you'll turn into one, you sissy!" called out Hiro, teasing Yoshio again.

"I'm not a sissy!" shouted Yoshio, getting quickly to his feet.

Masako wanted to step out from where she was hiding and give Hiro a piece of her mind. But she decided to wait for a moment first to see what Yoshio would do. From behind the wall, she watched Hiro as he came closer and closer to Hisako and her picture book, and she wondered whether he might take it away from her, or kick it, or do something else stupid. But before he could do anything, Yoshio launched himself at Hiro with tremendous force, sending him crashing over backwards on the ground.

"Be careful!" called out Masako, giving herself away and rushing over to where the two boys had landed.

Hiro was shocked to see her come out of nowhere and quickly got to his feet.

"You sissy!" he shouted one more time, then he ran off back home.

"Masako!" said Yoshio, brushing the dust off his clothes and running to his big sister, who got on her knees and swept him up in her arms.

"Are you okay?" asked Masako, amazed to see her little brother put up a fight. "You're not hurt, are you?"

"No, I'm fine!" said Yoshio in a surprisingly cheerful voice, then he gave her a little smile.

"Hee-hee," he giggled. "I just got in a fight!"

Masako hugged her little brother as hard as she could.

"Oh Yoshio," she said in a voice overflowing with kindness. "You're not supposed to fight! But I'm glad you did. My brave and tough little Yoshio!"